STAR WARS

EPISODE V
THE EMPIRE STRIKES BACK

VOLUME ONE

Script
ARCHIE GOODWIN

Art
AL WILLIAMSON

Art Assist
CARLOS GARZÓN

Colors
JAMES SINCLAIR

Lettering
RICK VEITCH

Cover Art
AL WILLIAMSON

Cover Colors
MATTHEW HOLLINGSWORTH

DARK HORSE COMICS

Spotlight

VISIT US AT
www.abdopublishing.com

Reinforced library bound edition published in 2010 by Spotlight, a division of the ABDO Group, 8000 West 78th Street, Edina, Minnesota 55439. Spotlight produces high-quality reinforced library bound editions for schools and libraries. Published by agreement with Dark Horse Comics, Inc., and Lucasfilm Ltd.

Printed in the United States of America, Melrose Park, Illinois.
092009
012010
♻ PRINTED ON RECYCLED PAPER

Library of Congress Cataloging-in-Publication Data

Goodwin, Archie.
  Episode V : the empire strikes back / based on the Screenplay by George Lucas ; script Adaptation Archie Goodwin ; artists Al Williamson & Carlos Garzon ; colorist James Sinclair ; letterer Rick Veitch. -- Reinforced library bound ed.
    p. cm. -- (Star Wars)
  "Dark Horse Comics."
  ISBN 978-1-59961-701-5 (vol. 1) -- ISBN 978-1-59961-702-2 (vol. 2) -- ISBN 978-1-59961-703-9 (vol. 3) -- ISBN 978-1-59961-704-6 (vol. 4)
  1. Graphic novels. [1. Graphic novels.] I. Lucas, George, 1944- II. Williamson, Al, 1931- III. Garzon, Carlos. IV. Empire strikes back (Motion Picture) V. Title. VI. Title: Episode five. VII. Title: Empire strikes back.
  PZ7.7.G656Epi 2010
  [Fic]--dc22

                                    2009030860

All Spotlight books have reinforced library bindings and are manufactured in the United States of America.

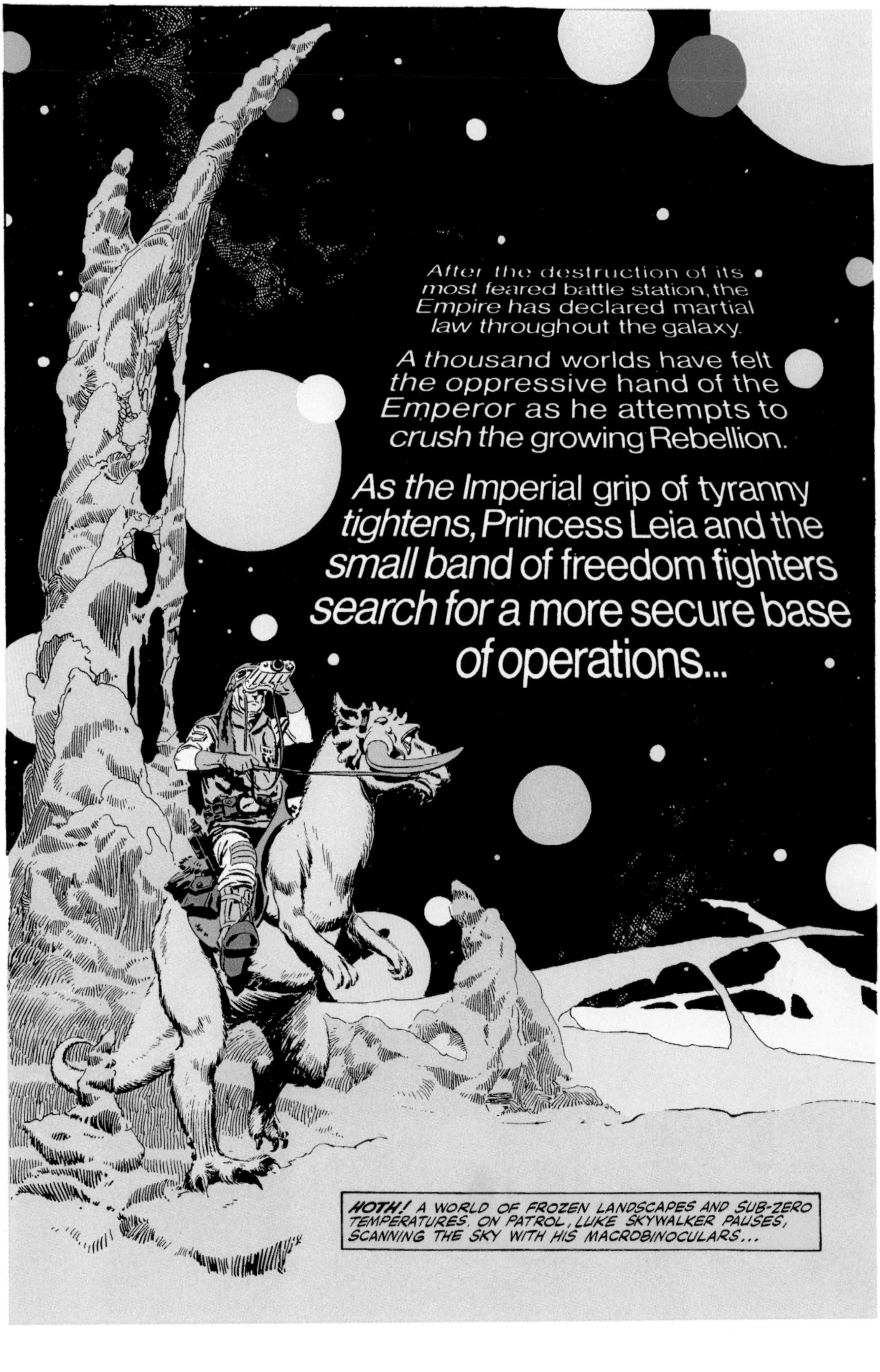
After the destruction of its most feared battle station, the Empire has declared martial law throughout the galaxy.
A thousand worlds have felt the oppressive hand of the Emperor as he attempts to crush the growing Rebellion.
As the Imperial grip of tyranny tightens, Princess Leia and the small band of freedom fighters search for a more secure base of operations...
HOTH! A WORLD OF FROZEN LANDSCAPES AND SUB-ZERO TEMPERATURES. ON PATROL, LUKE SKYWALKER PAUSES, SCANNING THE SKY WITH HIS MACROBINOCULARS...

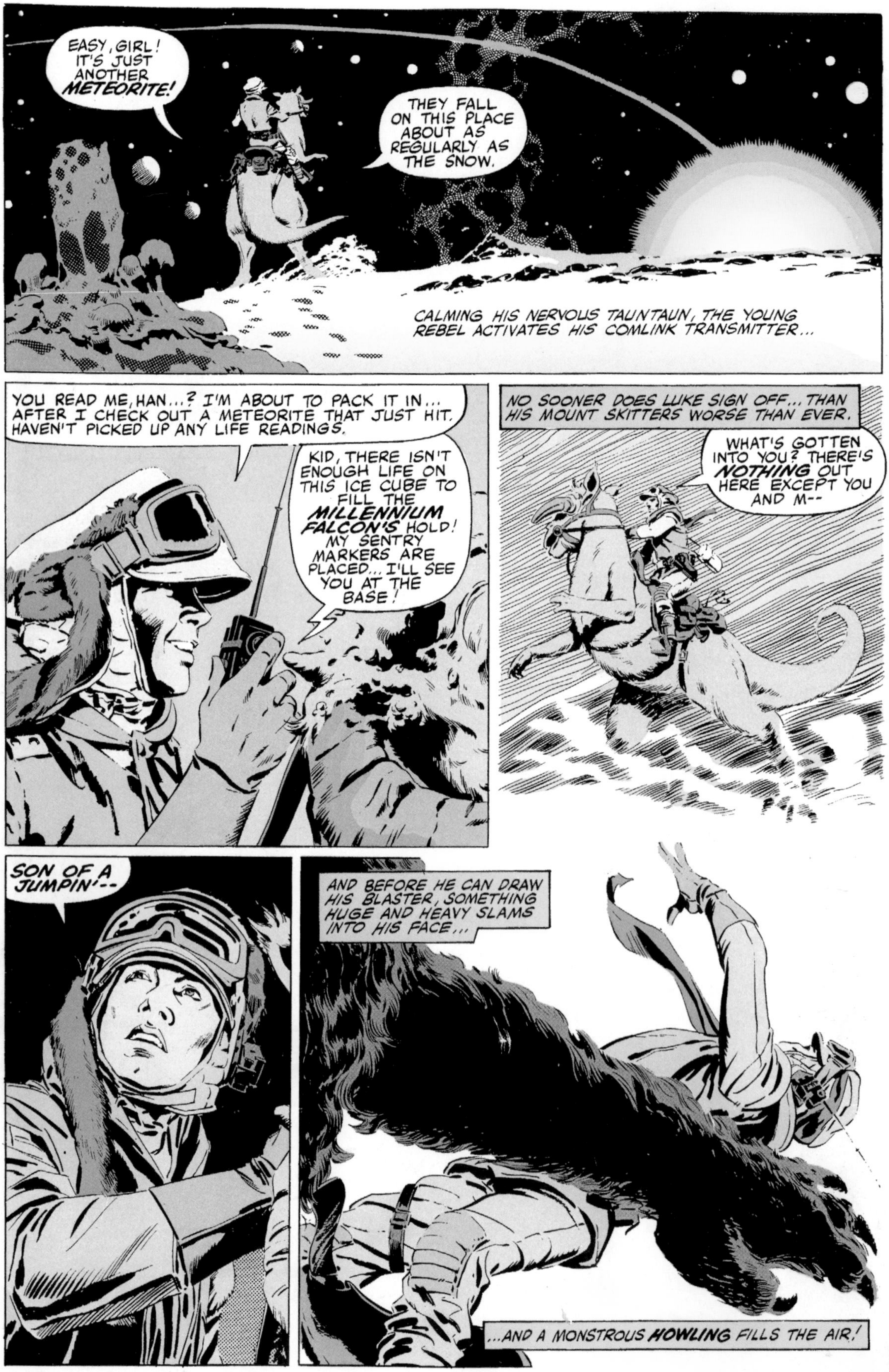
EASY, GIRL! IT'S JUST ANOTHER METEORITE!
THEY FALL ON THIS PLACE ABOUT AS REGULARLY AS THE SNOW.
CALMING HIS NERVOUS TAUNTAUN, THE YOUNG REBEL ACTIVATES HIS COMLINK TRANSMITTER...
YOU READ ME, HAN...? I'M ABOUT TO PACK IT IN... AFTER I CHECK OUT A METEORITE THAT JUST HIT. HAVEN'T PICKED UP ANY LIFE READINGS.
KID, THERE ISN'T ENOUGH LIFE ON THIS ICE CUBE TO FILL THE MILLENNIUM FALCON'S HOLD! MY SENTRY MARKERS ARE PLACED... I'LL SEE YOU AT THE BASE!
NO SOONER DOES LUKE SIGN OFF... THAN HIS MOUNT SKITTERS WORSE THAN EVER.
WHAT'S GOTTEN INTO YOU? THERE'S NOTHING OUT HERE EXCEPT YOU AND M--
SON OF A JUMPIN'--
AND BEFORE HE CAN DRAW HIS BLASTER, SOMETHING HUGE AND HEAVY SLAMS INTO HIS FACE...
...AND A MONSTROUS HOWLING FILLS THE AIR!

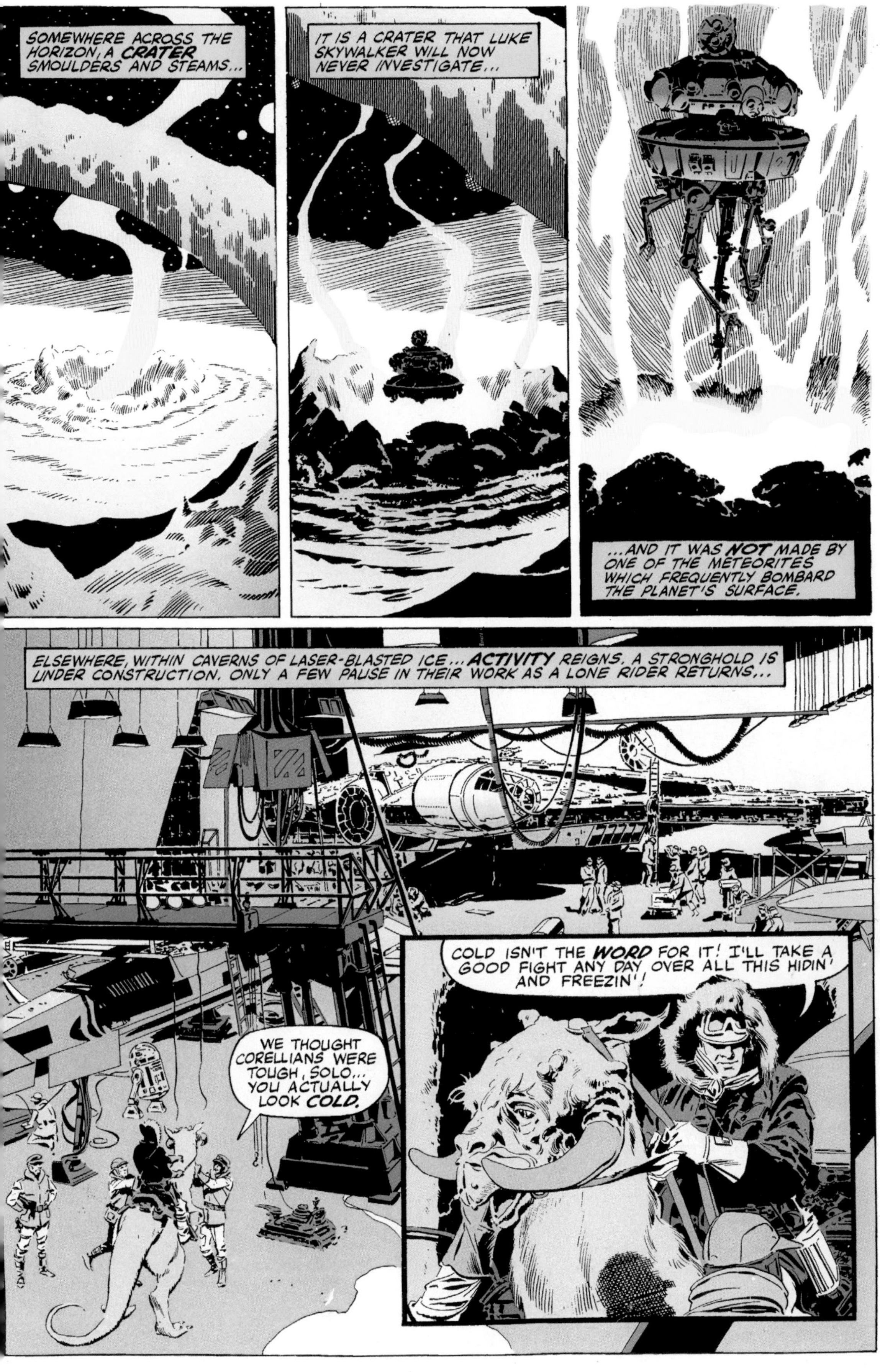
SOMEWHERE ACROSS THE HORIZON, A CRATER SMOULDERS AND STEAMS...
IT IS A CRATER THAT LUKE SKYWALKER WILL NOW NEVER INVESTIGATE...
...AND IT WAS NOT MADE BY ONE OF THE METEORITES WHICH FREQUENTLY BOMBARD THE PLANET'S SURFACE.
ELSEWHERE, WITHIN CAVERNS OF LASER-BLASTED ICE... ACTIVITY REIGNS. A STRONGHOLD IS UNDER CONSTRUCTION. ONLY A FEW PAUSE IN THEIR WORK AS A LONE RIDER RETURNS...
WE THOUGHT CORELLIANS WERE TOUGH, SOLO... YOU ACTUALLY LOOK COLD.
COLD ISN'T THE WORD FOR IT! I'LL TAKE A GOOD FIGHT ANY DAY OVER ALL THIS HIDIN' AND FREEZIN'!

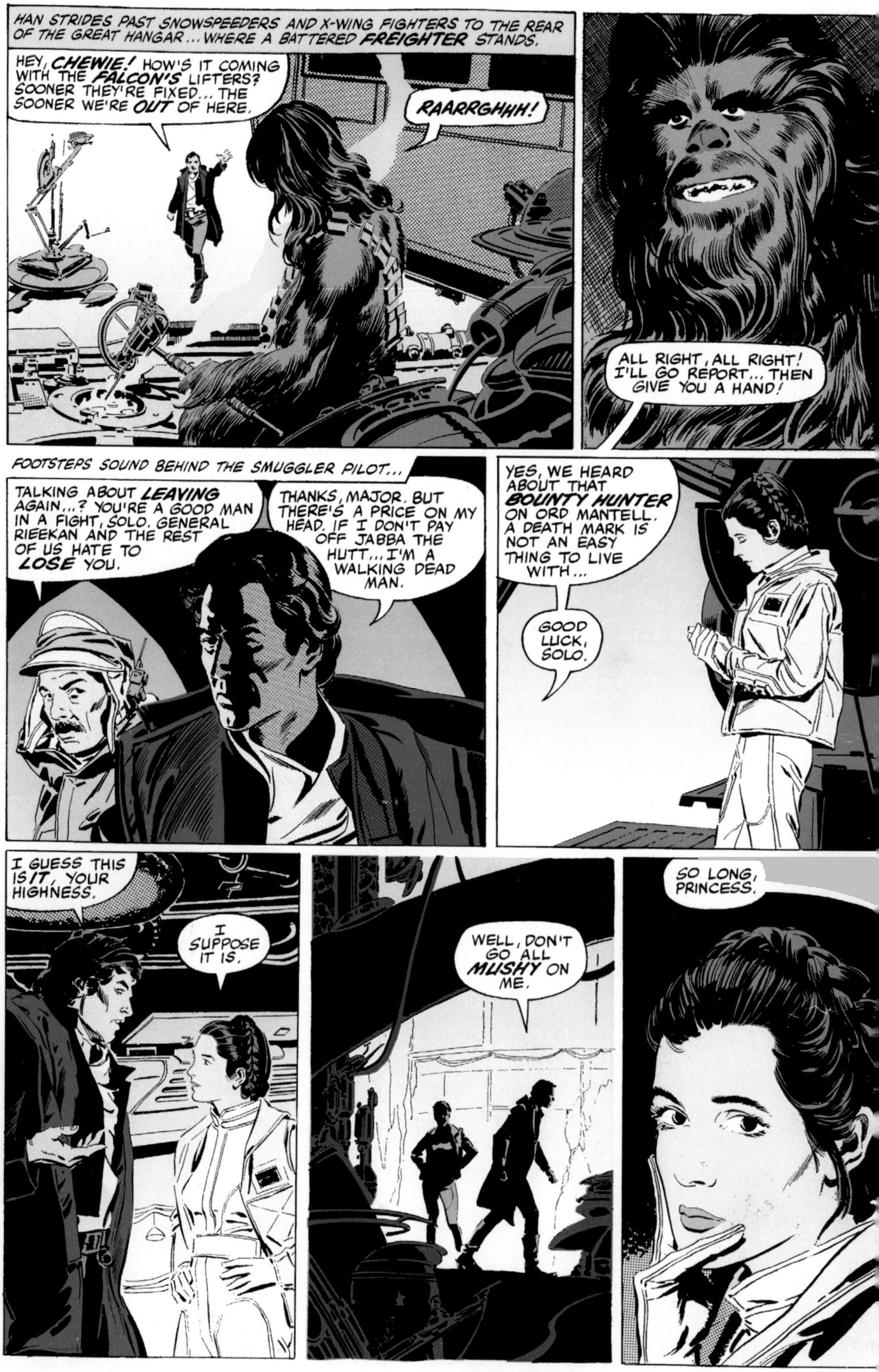
HAN STRIDES PAST SNOWSPEEDERS AND X-WING FIGHTERS TO THE REAR OF THE GREAT HANGAR... WHERE A BATTERED FREIGHTER STANDS.
HEY, CHEWIE! HOW'S IT COMING WITH THE FALCON'S LIFTERS? SOONER THEY'RE FIXED... THE SOONER WE'RE OUT OF HERE.
RAARRGHHH!
ALL RIGHT, ALL RIGHT! I'LL GO REPORT... THEN GIVE YOU A HAND!
FOOTSTEPS SOUND BEHIND THE SMUGGLER PILOT...
TALKING ABOUT LEAVING AGAIN...? YOU'RE A GOOD MAN IN A FIGHT, SOLO. GENERAL RIEEKAN AND THE REST OF US HATE TO LOSE YOU.
THANKS, MAJOR. BUT THERE'S A PRICE ON MY HEAD. IF I DON'T PAY OFF JABBA THE HUTT... I'M A WALKING DEAD MAN.
YES, WE HEARD ABOUT THAT BOUNTY HUNTER ON ORD MANTELL. A DEATH MARK IS NOT AN EASY THING TO LIVE WITH...
GOOD LUCK, SOLO.
I GUESS THIS IS IT, YOUR HIGHNESS.
I SUPPOSE IT IS.
WELL, DON'T GO ALL MUSHY ON ME.
SO LONG, PRINCESS.

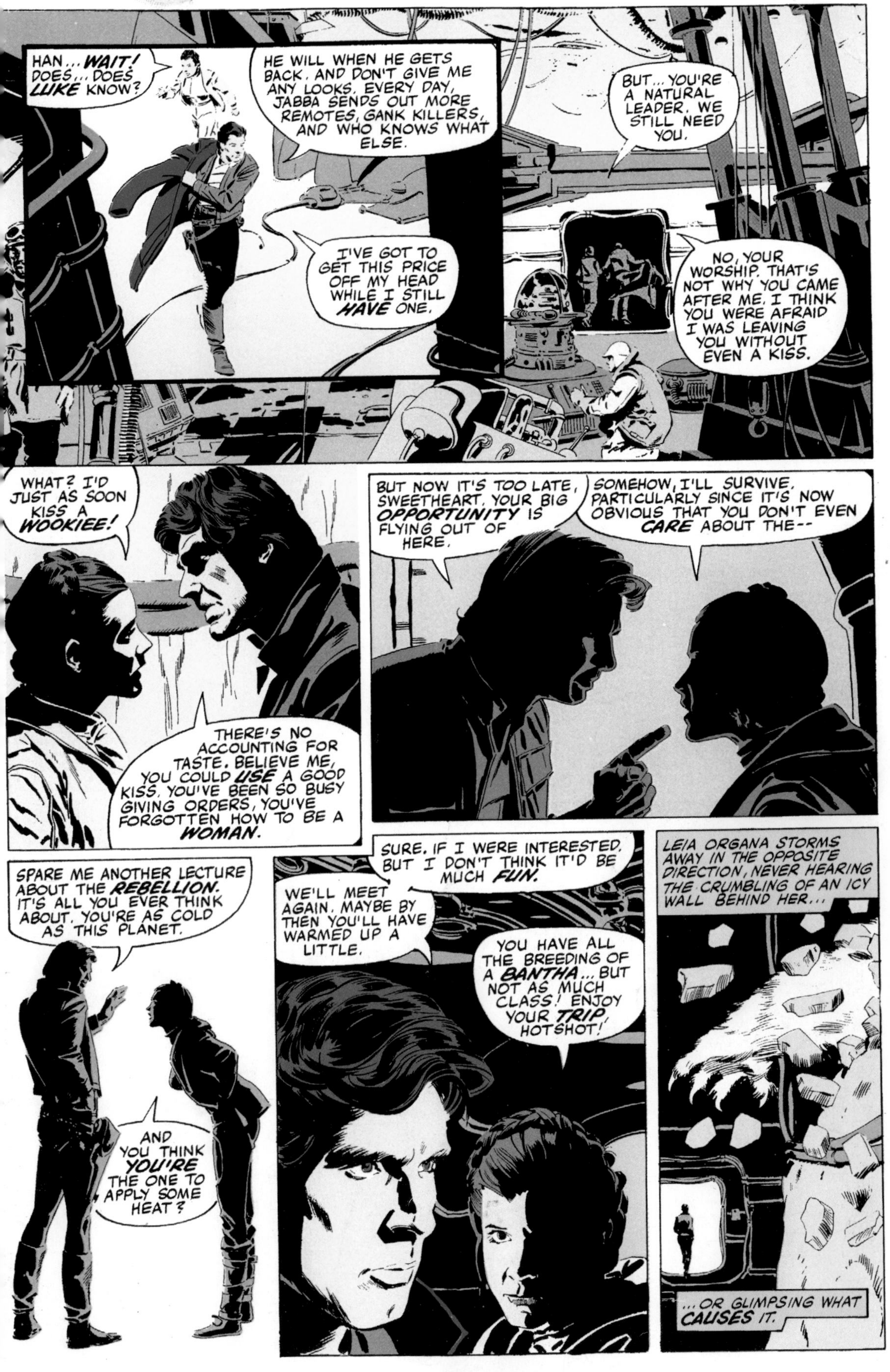
HAN... WAIT! DOES... DOES LUKE KNOW?
HE WILL WHEN HE GETS BACK. AND DON'T GIVE ME ANY LOOKS. EVERY DAY, JABBA SENDS OUT MORE REMOTES, GANK KILLERS, AND WHO KNOWS WHAT ELSE.
I'VE GOT TO GET THIS PRICE OFF MY HEAD WHILE I STILL HAVE ONE.
BUT... YOU'RE A NATURAL LEADER. WE STILL NEED YOU.
NO, YOUR WORSHIP. THAT'S NOT WHY YOU CAME AFTER ME. I THINK YOU WERE AFRAID I WAS LEAVING YOU WITHOUT EVEN A KISS.
WHAT? I'D JUST AS SOON KISS A WOOKIEE!
THERE'S NO ACCOUNTING FOR TASTE. BELIEVE ME, YOU COULD USE A GOOD KISS. YOU'VE BEEN SO BUSY GIVING ORDERS, YOU'VE FORGOTTEN HOW TO BE A WOMAN.
BUT NOW IT'S TOO LATE, SWEETHEART. YOUR BIG OPPORTUNITY IS FLYING OUT OF HERE.
SOMEHOW, I'LL SURVIVE, PARTICULARLY SINCE IT'S NOW OBVIOUS THAT YOU DON'T EVEN CARE ABOUT THE--
SPARE ME ANOTHER LECTURE ABOUT THE REBELLION. IT'S ALL YOU EVER THINK ABOUT. YOU'RE AS COLD AS THIS PLANET.
AND YOU THINK YOU'RE THE ONE TO APPLY SOME HEAT?
SURE, IF I WERE INTERESTED. BUT I DON'T THINK IT'D BE MUCH FUN.
WE'LL MEET AGAIN. MAYBE BY THEN YOU'LL HAVE WARMED UP A LITTLE.
YOU HAVE ALL THE BREEDING OF A BANTHA... BUT NOT AS MUCH CLASS! ENJOY YOUR TRIP, HOTSHOT!
LEIA ORGANA STORMS AWAY IN THE OPPOSITE DIRECTION, NEVER HEARING THE CRUMBLING OF AN ICY WALL BEHIND HER...
...OR GLIMPSING WHAT CAUSES IT.

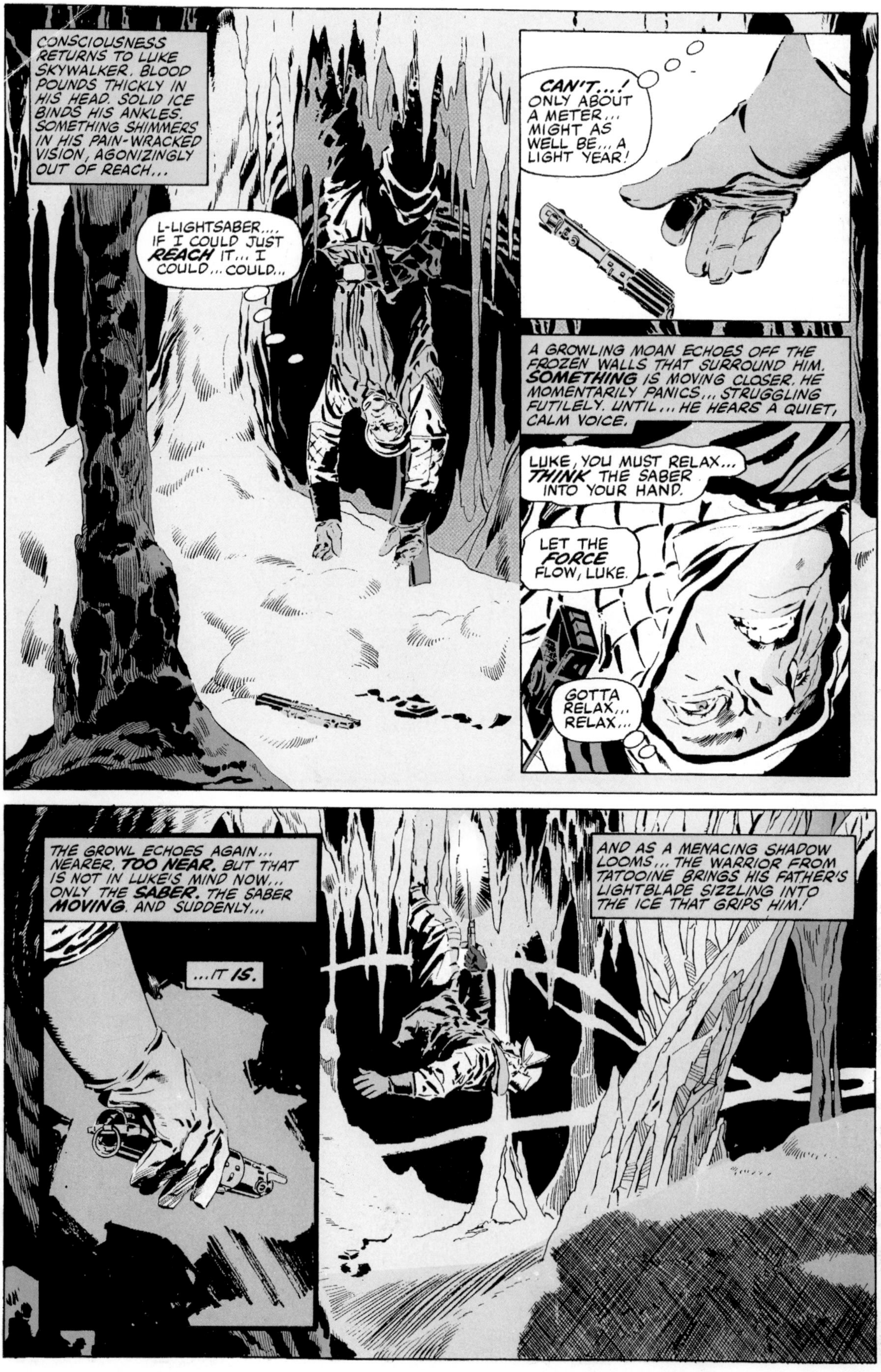
CONSCIOUSNESS RETURNS TO LUKE SKYWALKER. BLOOD POUNDS THICKLY IN HIS HEAD. SOLID ICE BINDS HIS ANKLES. SOMETHING SHIMMERS IN HIS PAIN-WRACKED VISION, AGONIZINGLY OUT OF REACH...
L-LIGHTSABER.... IF I COULD JUST REACH IT... I COULD... COULD...
CAN'T...! ONLY ABOUT A METER... MIGHT AS WELL BE... A LIGHT YEAR!
A GROWLING MOAN ECHOES OFF THE FROZEN WALLS THAT SURROUND HIM. SOMETHING IS MOVING CLOSER. HE MOMENTARILY PANICS... STRUGGLING FUTILELY. UNTIL... HE HEARS A QUIET, CALM VOICE.
LUKE, YOU MUST RELAX... THINK THE SABER INTO YOUR HAND.
LET THE FORCE FLOW, LUKE.
GOTTA RELAX... RELAX...
THE GROWL ECHOES AGAIN... NEARER. TOO NEAR. BUT THAT IS NOT IN LUKE'S MIND NOW... ONLY THE SABER. THE SABER MOVING. AND SUDDENLY...
...IT IS.
AND AS A MENACING SHADOW LOOMS... THE WARRIOR FROM TATOOINE BRINGS HIS FATHER'S LIGHTBLADE SIZZLING INTO THE ICE THAT GRIPS HIM!

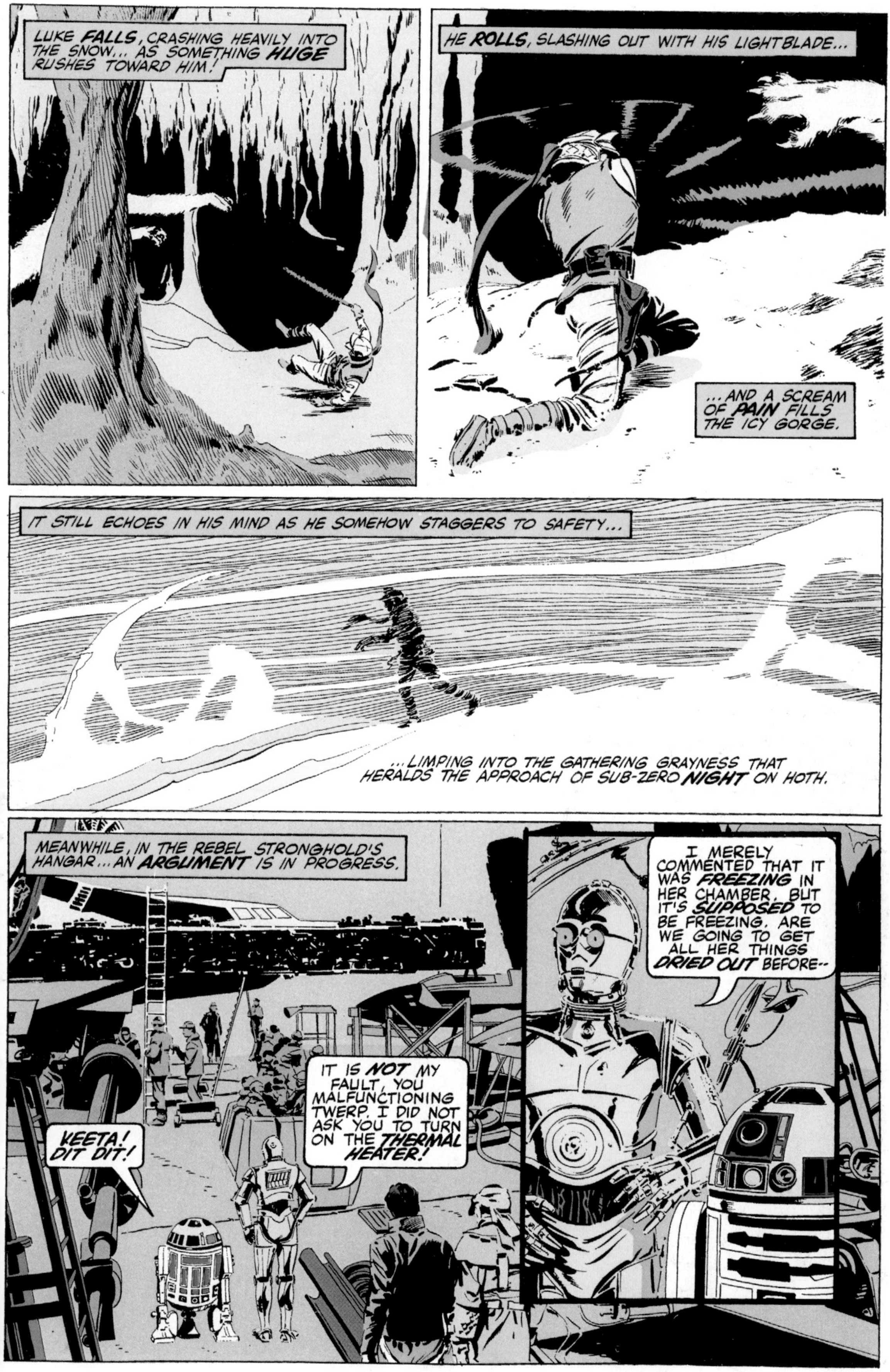
LUKE FALLS, CRASHING HEAVILY INTO THE SNOW... AS SOMETHING HUGE RUSHES TOWARD HIM!
HE ROLLS, SLASHING OUT WITH HIS LIGHTBLADE...
...AND A SCREAM OF PAIN FILLS THE ICY GORGE.
IT STILL ECHOES IN HIS MIND AS HE SOMEHOW STAGGERS TO SAFETY...
...LIMPING INTO THE GATHERING GRAYNESS THAT HERALDS THE APPROACH OF SUB-ZERO NIGHT ON HOTH.
MEANWHILE, IN THE REBEL STRONGHOLD'S HANGAR... AN ARGUMENT IS IN PROGRESS.
KEETA! DIT DIT!
IT IS NOT MY FAULT, YOU MALFUNCTIONING TWERP. I DID NOT ASK YOU TO TURN ON THE THERMAL HEATER!
I MERELY COMMENTED THAT IT WAS FREEZING IN HER CHAMBER. BUT IT'S SUPPOSED TO BE FREEZING. ARE WE GOING TO GET ALL HER THINGS DRIED OUT BEFORE--

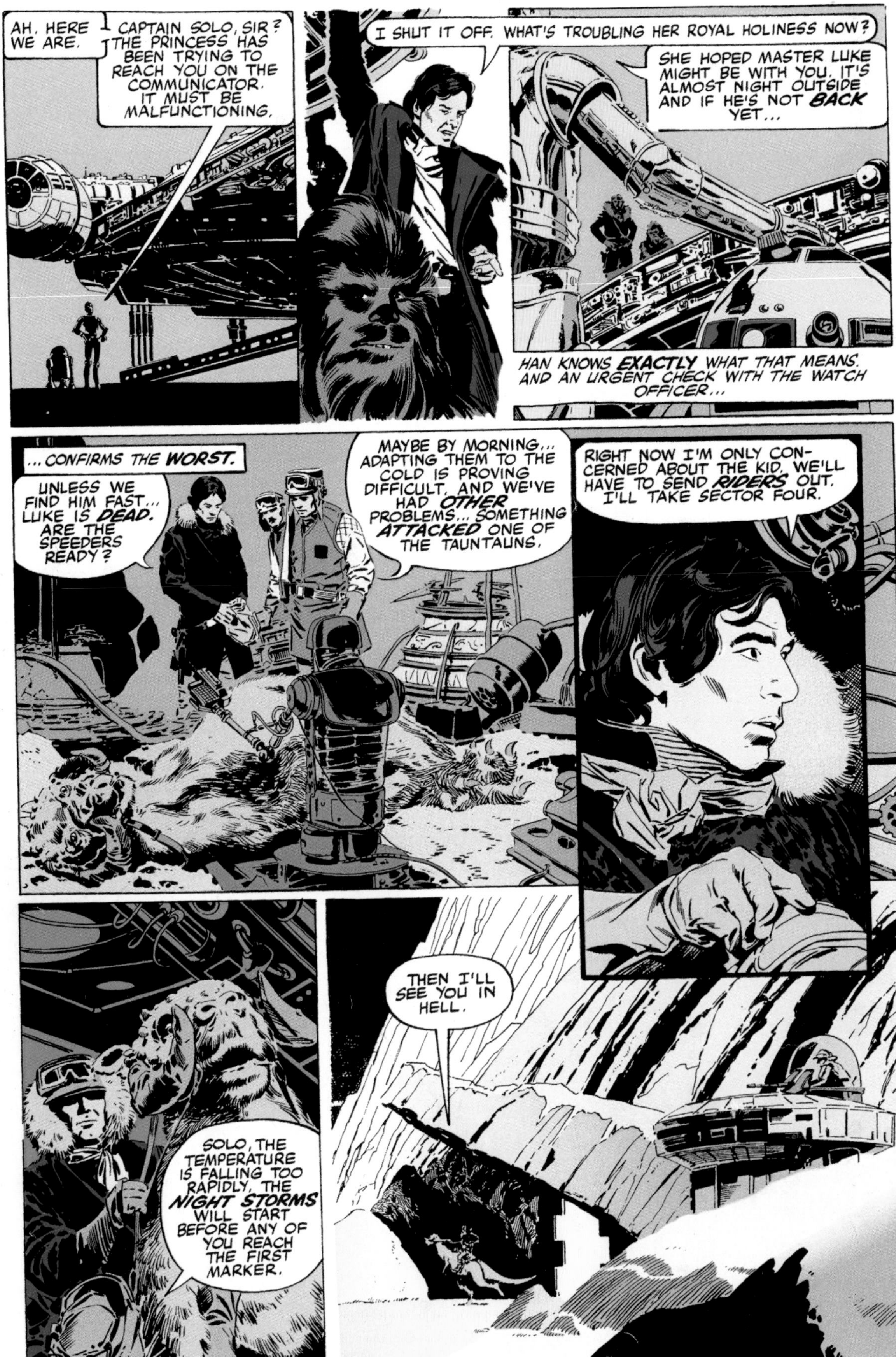
AH, HERE WE ARE.
CAPTAIN SOLO, SIR? THE PRINCESS HAS BEEN TRYING TO REACH YOU ON THE COMMUNICATOR. IT MUST BE MALFUNCTIONING.
I SHUT IT OFF. WHAT'S TROUBLING HER ROYAL HOLINESS NOW?
SHE HOPED MASTER LUKE MIGHT BE WITH YOU. IT'S ALMOST NIGHT OUTSIDE AND IF HE'S NOT BACK YET...
HAN KNOWS EXACTLY WHAT THAT MEANS. AND AN URGENT CHECK WITH THE WATCH OFFICER...
...CONFIRMS THE WORST.
UNLESS WE FIND HIM FAST... LUKE IS DEAD. ARE THE SPEEDERS READY?
MAYBE BY MORNING... ADAPTING THEM TO THE COLD IS PROVING DIFFICULT, AND WE'VE HAD OTHER PROBLEMS... SOMETHING ATTACKED ONE OF THE TAUNTAUNS.
RIGHT NOW I'M ONLY CONCERNED ABOUT THE KID. WE'LL HAVE TO SEND RIDERS OUT. I'LL TAKE SECTOR FOUR.
SOLO, THE TEMPERATURE IS FALLING TOO RAPIDLY. THE NIGHT STORMS WILL START BEFORE ANY OF YOU REACH THE FIRST MARKER.
THEN I'LL SEE YOU IN HELL.

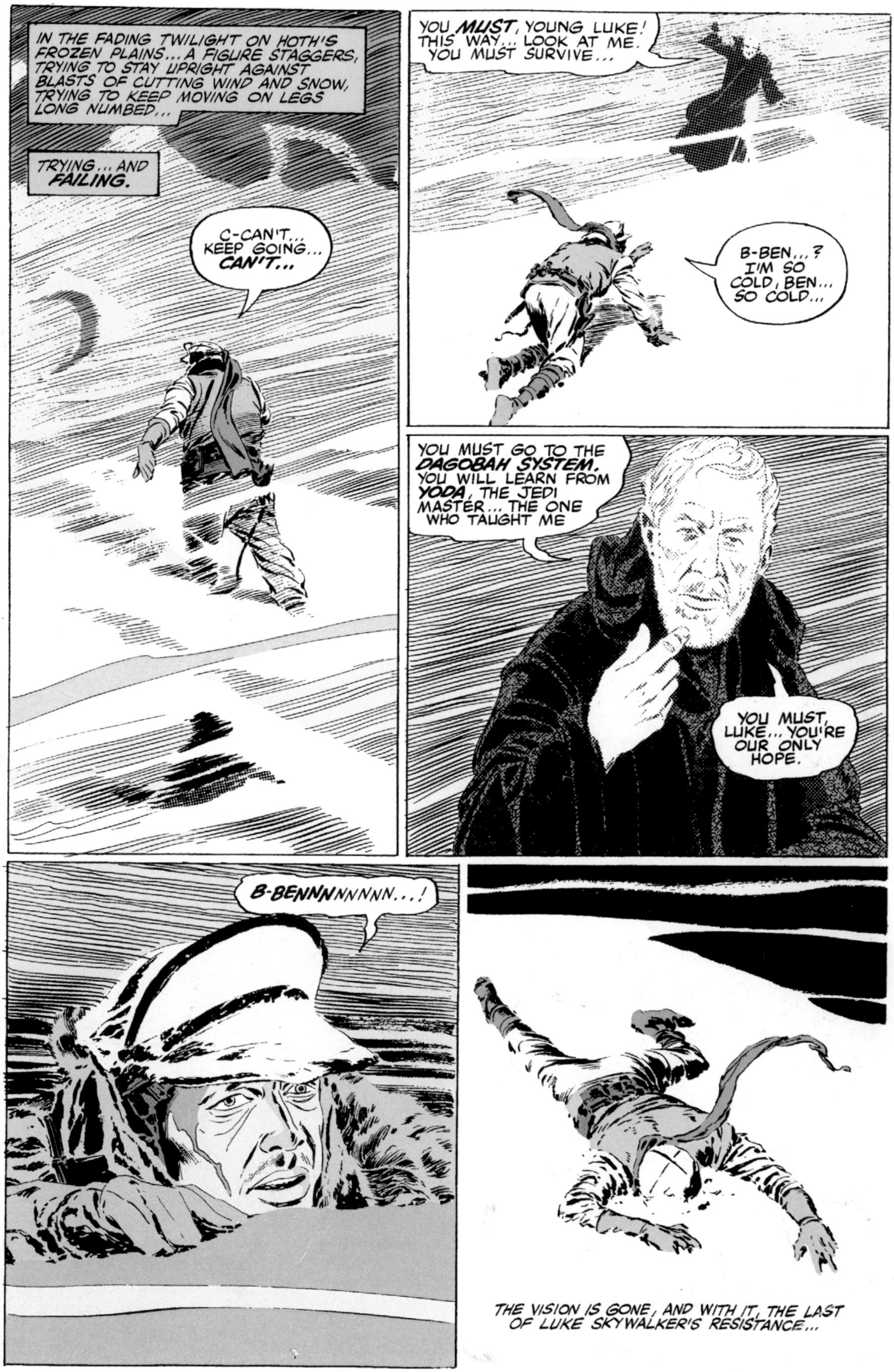
IN THE FADING TWILIGHT ON HOTH'S FROZEN PLAINS... A FIGURE STAGGERS, TRYING TO STAY UPRIGHT AGAINST BLASTS OF CUTTING WIND AND SNOW, TRYING TO KEEP MOVING ON LEGS LONG NUMBED...
TRYING... AND FAILING.
C-CAN'T... KEEP GOING... CAN'T...
YOU MUST, YOUNG LUKE! THIS WAY... LOOK AT ME. YOU MUST SURVIVE...
B-BEN...? I'M SO COLD, BEN... SO COLD...
YOU MUST GO TO THE DAGOBAH SYSTEM. YOU WILL LEARN FROM YODA, THE JEDI MASTER... THE ONE WHO TAUGHT ME
YOU MUST, LUKE... YOU'RE OUR ONLY HOPE.
B-BENNNNNNNN...!
THE VISION IS GONE, AND WITH IT, THE LAST OF LUKE SKYWALKER'S RESISTANCE...

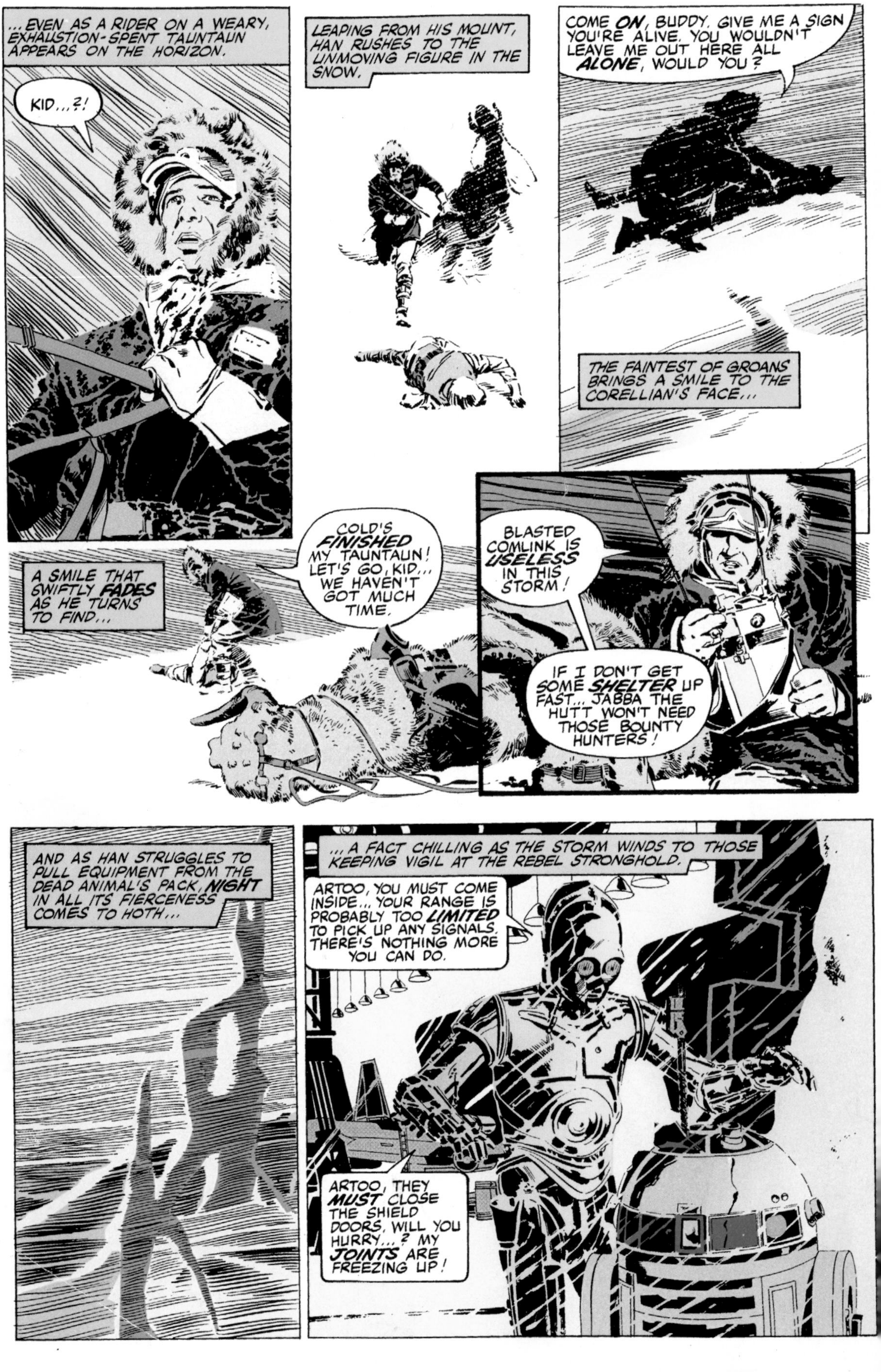

...EVEN AS A RIDER ON A WEARY, EXHAUSTION-SPENT TAUNTAUN APPEARS ON THE HORIZON.
KID...?!
LEAPING FROM HIS MOUNT, HAN RUSHES TO THE UNMOVING FIGURE IN THE SNOW.
COME ON, BUDDY. GIVE ME A SIGN YOU'RE ALIVE. YOU WOULDN'T LEAVE ME OUT HERE ALL ALONE, WOULD YOU?
THE FAINTEST OF GROANS BRINGS A SMILE TO THE CORELLIAN'S FACE...
A SMILE THAT SWIFTLY FADES AS HE TURNS TO FIND...
COLD'S FINISHED MY TAUNTAUN! LET'S GO, KID... WE HAVEN'T GOT MUCH TIME.
BLASTED COMLINK IS USELESS IN THIS STORM!
IF I DON'T GET SOME SHELTER UP FAST... JABBA THE HUTT WON'T NEED THOSE BOUNTY HUNTERS!
AND AS HAN STRUGGLES TO PULL EQUIPMENT FROM THE DEAD ANIMAL'S PACK, NIGHT IN ALL ITS FIERCENESS COMES TO HOTH...
...A FACT CHILLING AS THE STORM WINDS TO THOSE KEEPING VIGIL AT THE REBEL STRONGHOLD.
ARTOO, YOU MUST COME INSIDE... YOUR RANGE IS PROBABLY TOO LIMITED TO PICK UP ANY SIGNALS. THERE'S NOTHING MORE YOU CAN DO.
ARTOO, THEY MUST CLOSE THE SHIELD DOORS. WILL YOU HURRY...? MY JOINTS ARE FREEZING UP!

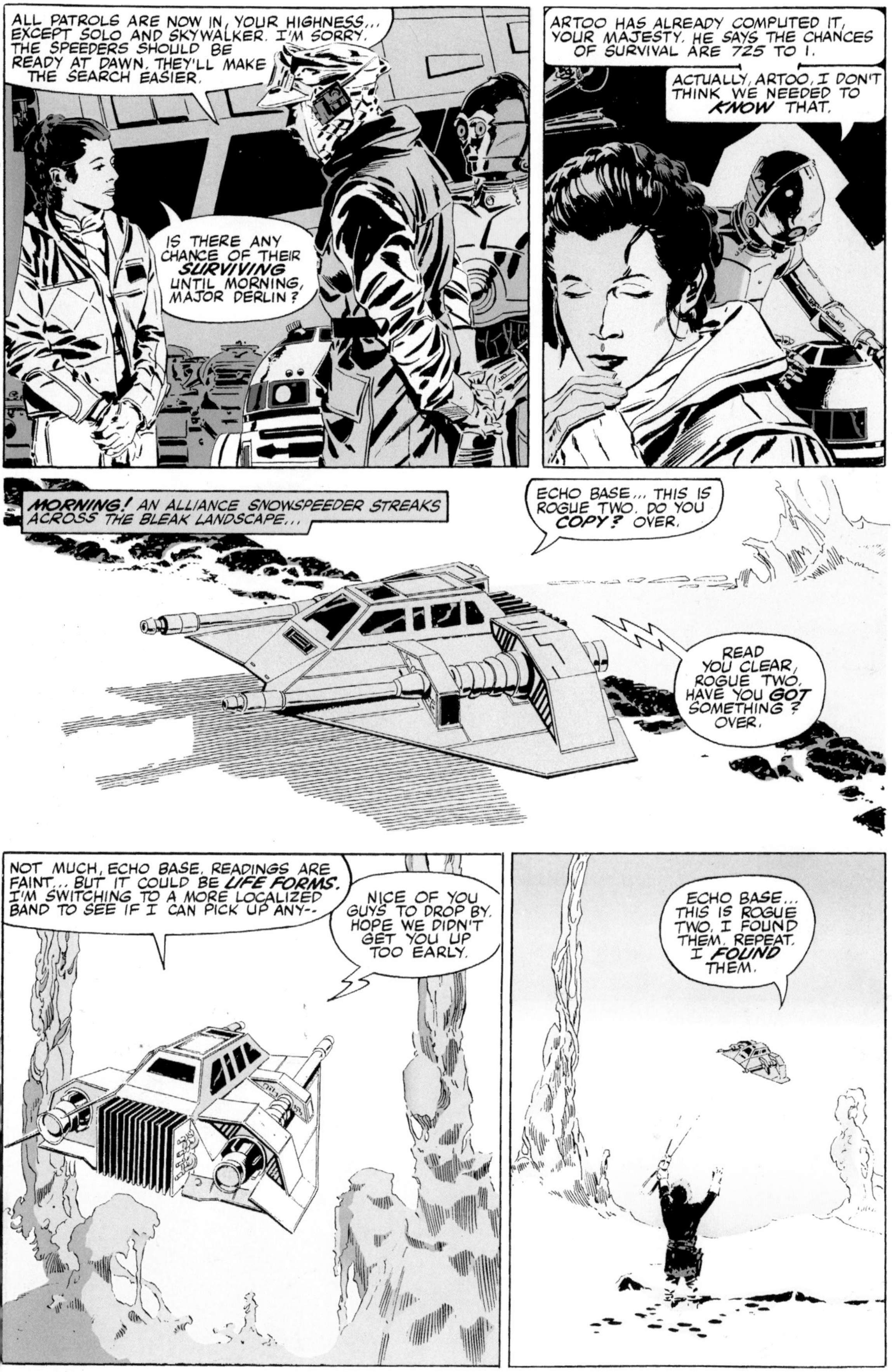
ALL PATROLS ARE NOW IN, YOUR HIGHNESS... EXCEPT SOLO AND SKYWALKER. I'M SORRY. THE SPEEDERS SHOULD BE READY AT DAWN. THEY'LL MAKE THE SEARCH EASIER.
IS THERE ANY CHANCE OF THEIR SURVIVING UNTIL MORNING, MAJOR DERLIN?
ARTOO HAS ALREADY COMPUTED IT, YOUR MAJESTY. HE SAYS THE CHANCES OF SURVIVAL ARE 725 TO 1.
ACTUALLY, ARTOO, I DON'T THINK WE NEEDED TO KNOW THAT.
MORNING! AN ALLIANCE SNOWSPEEDER STREAKS ACROSS THE BLEAK LANDSCAPE...
ECHO BASE... THIS IS ROGUE TWO. DO YOU COPY? OVER.
READ YOU CLEAR, ROGUE TWO. HAVE YOU GOT SOMETHING? OVER.
NOT MUCH, ECHO BASE. READINGS ARE FAINT... BUT IT COULD BE LIFE FORMS. I'M SWITCHING TO A MORE LOCALIZED BAND TO SEE IF I CAN PICK UP ANY--
NICE OF YOU GUYS TO DROP BY. HOPE WE DIDN'T GET YOU UP TOO EARLY.
ECHO BASE... THIS IS ROGUE TWO. I FOUND THEM. REPEAT. I FOUND THEM.

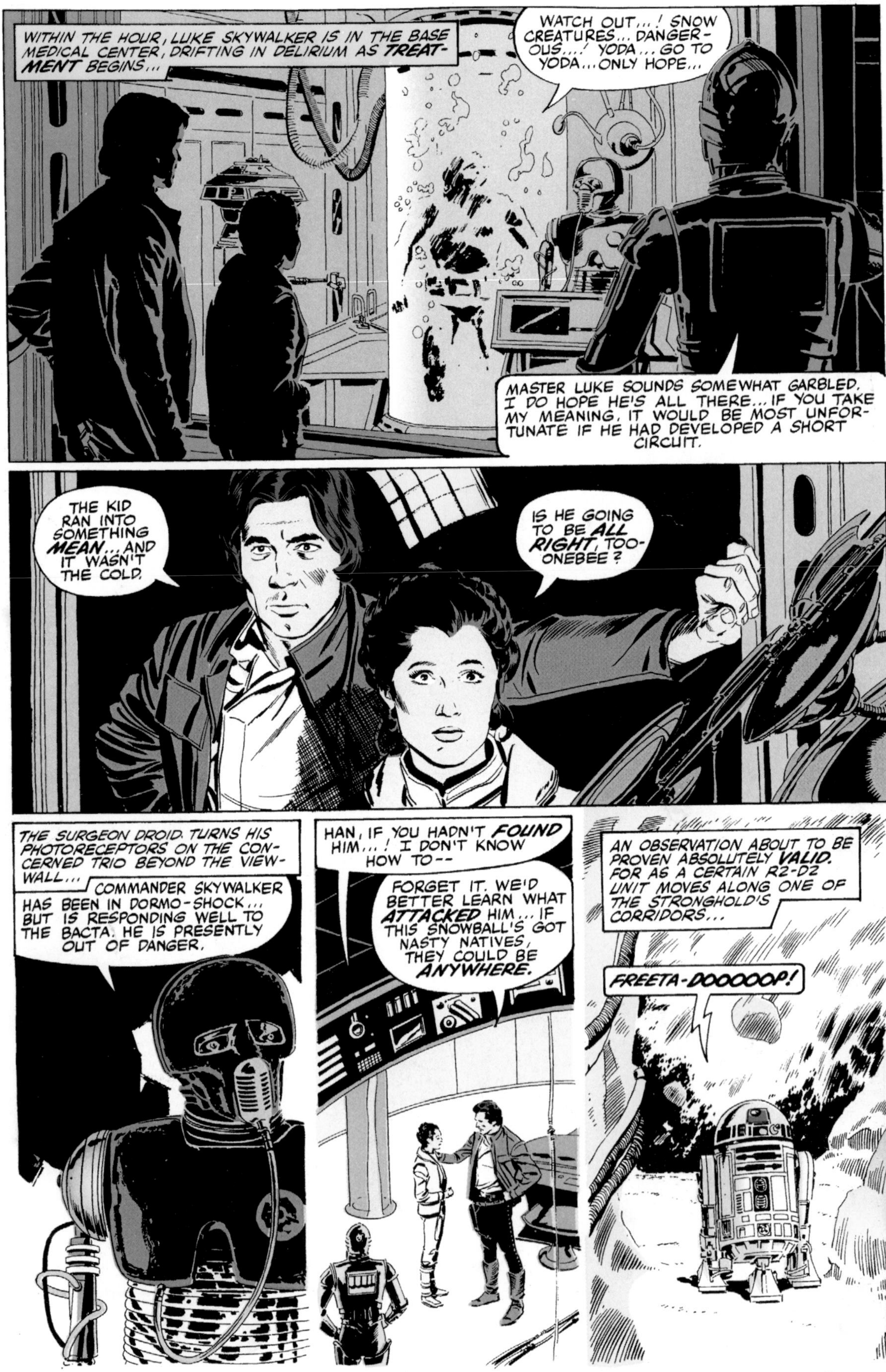
WITHIN THE HOUR, LUKE SKYWALKER IS IN THE BASE MEDICAL CENTER, DRIFTING IN DELIRIUM AS TREATMENT BEGINS...
WATCH OUT...! SNOW CREATURES... DANGEROUS...! YODA... GO TO YODA... ONLY HOPE...
MASTER LUKE SOUNDS SOMEWHAT GARBLED. I DO HOPE HE'S ALL THERE... IF YOU TAKE MY MEANING. IT WOULD BE MOST UNFORTUNATE IF HE HAD DEVELOPED A SHORT CIRCUIT.
THE KID RAN INTO SOMETHING MEAN... AND IT WASN'T THE COLD.
IS HE GOING TO BE ALL RIGHT, TOO-ONEBEE?
THE SURGEON DROID TURNS HIS PHOTORECEPTORS ON THE CONCERNED TRIO BEYOND THE VIEW-WALL...
COMMANDER SKYWALKER HAS BEEN IN DORMO-SHOCK... BUT IS RESPONDING WELL TO THE BACTA. HE IS PRESENTLY OUT OF DANGER.
HAN, IF YOU HADN'T FOUND HIM...! I DON'T KNOW HOW TO--
FORGET IT. WE'D BETTER LEARN WHAT ATTACKED HIM... IF THIS SNOWBALL'S GOT NASTY NATIVES, THEY COULD BE ANYWHERE.
AN OBSERVATION ABOUT TO BE PROVEN ABSOLUTELY VALID. FOR AS A CERTAIN R2-D2 UNIT MOVES ALONG ONE OF THE STRONGHOLD'S CORRIDORS...
FREETA-DOOOOOP!

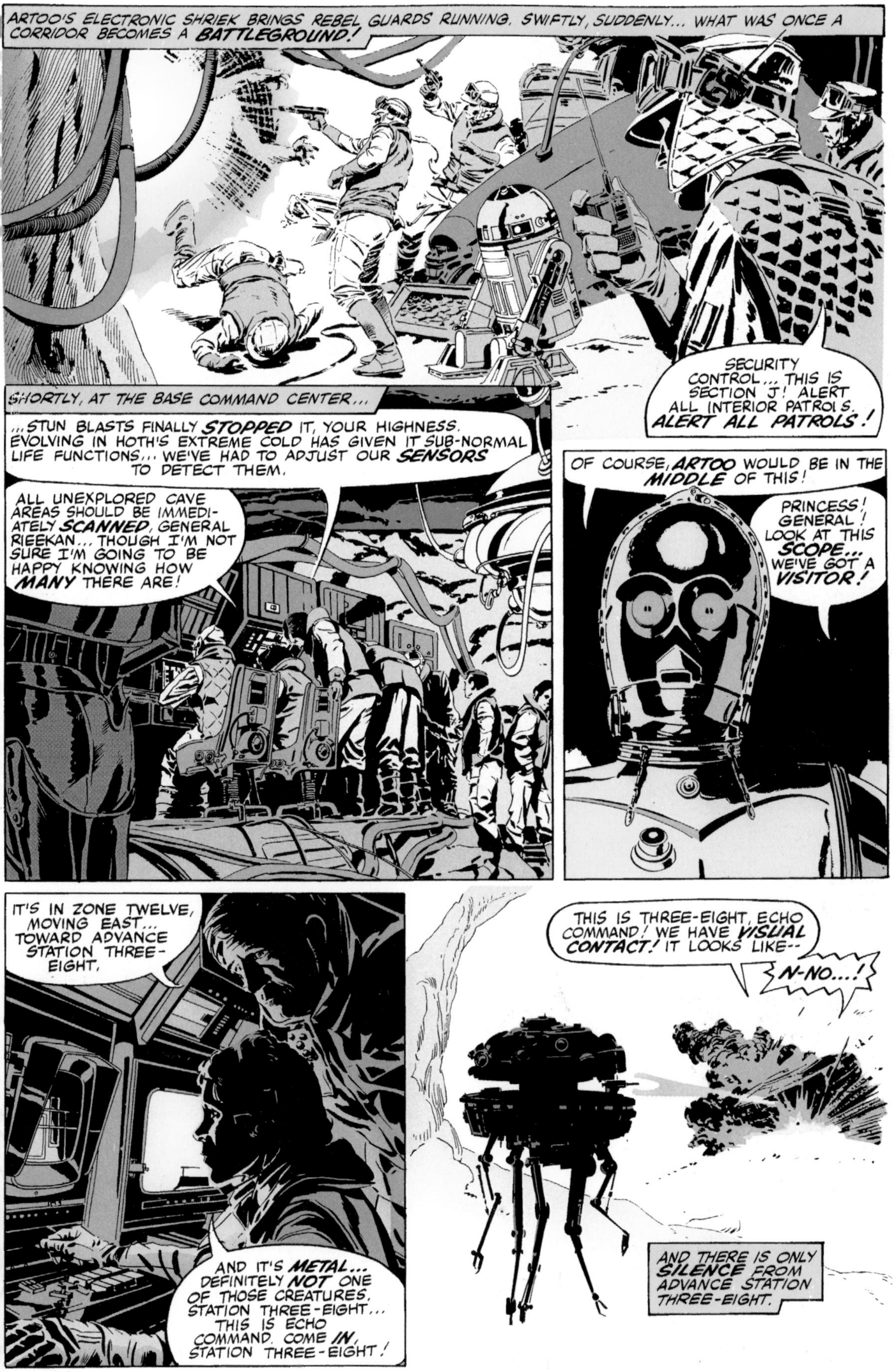
ARTOO'S ELECTRONIC SHRIEK BRINGS REBEL GUARDS RUNNING. SWIFTLY, SUDDENLY... WHAT WAS ONCE A CORRIDOR BECOMES A BATTLEGROUND!
SECURITY CONTROL... THIS IS SECTION J! ALERT ALL INTERIOR PATROLS. ALERT ALL PATROLS!
SHORTLY, AT THE BASE COMMAND CENTER...
...STUN BLASTS FINALLY STOPPED IT, YOUR HIGHNESS. EVOLVING IN HOTH'S EXTREME COLD HAS GIVEN IT SUB-NORMAL LIFE FUNCTIONS... WE'VE HAD TO ADJUST OUR SENSORS TO DETECT THEM.
ALL UNEXPLORED CAVE AREAS SHOULD BE IMMEDIATELY SCANNED, GENERAL RIEEKAN... THOUGH I'M NOT SURE I'M GOING TO BE HAPPY KNOWING HOW MANY THERE ARE!
OF COURSE, ARTOO WOULD BE IN THE MIDDLE OF THIS!
PRINCESS! GENERAL! LOOK AT THIS SCOPE... WE'VE GOT A VISITOR!
IT'S IN ZONE TWELVE, MOVING EAST... TOWARD ADVANCE STATION THREE-EIGHT.
AND IT'S METAL... DEFINITELY NOT ONE OF THOSE CREATURES. STATION THREE-EIGHT... THIS IS ECHO COMMAND. COME IN, STATION THREE-EIGHT!
THIS IS THREE-EIGHT, ECHO COMMAND! WE HAVE VISUAL CONTACT! IT LOOKS LIKE--
N-NO...!
AND THERE IS ONLY SILENCE FROM ADVANCE STATION THREE-EIGHT.

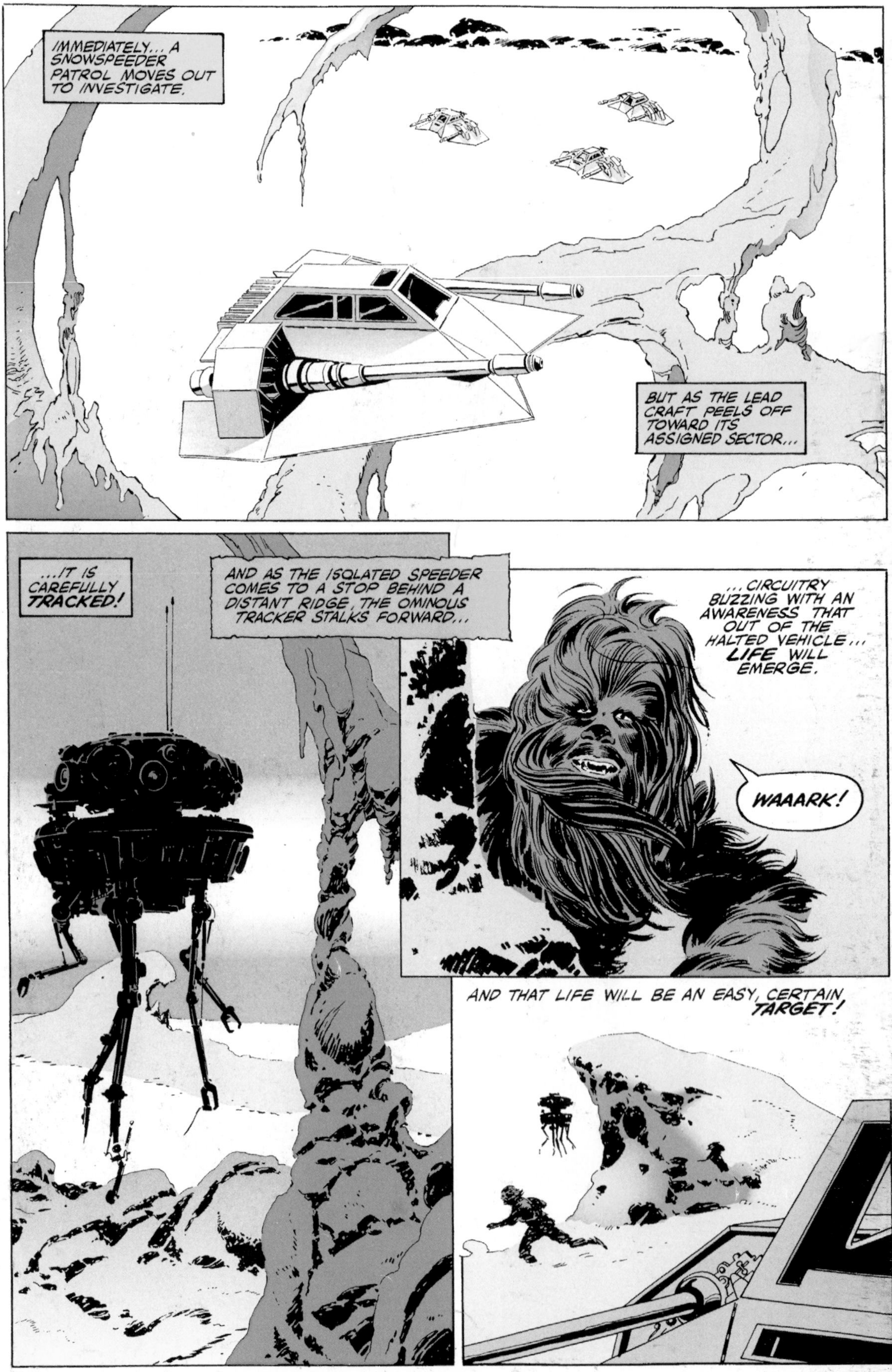
IMMEDIATELY... A SNOWSPEEDER PATROL MOVES OUT TO INVESTIGATE.
BUT AS THE LEAD CRAFT PEELS OFF TOWARD ITS ASSIGNED SECTOR...
...IT IS CAREFULLY TRACKED!
AND AS THE ISOLATED SPEEDER COMES TO A STOP BEHIND A DISTANT RIDGE, THE OMINOUS TRACKER STALKS FORWARD...
...CIRCUITRY BUZZING WITH AN AWARENESS THAT OUT OF THE HALTED VEHICLE... LIFE WILL EMERGE.
WAAARK!
AND THAT LIFE WILL BE AN EASY, CERTAIN TARGET!

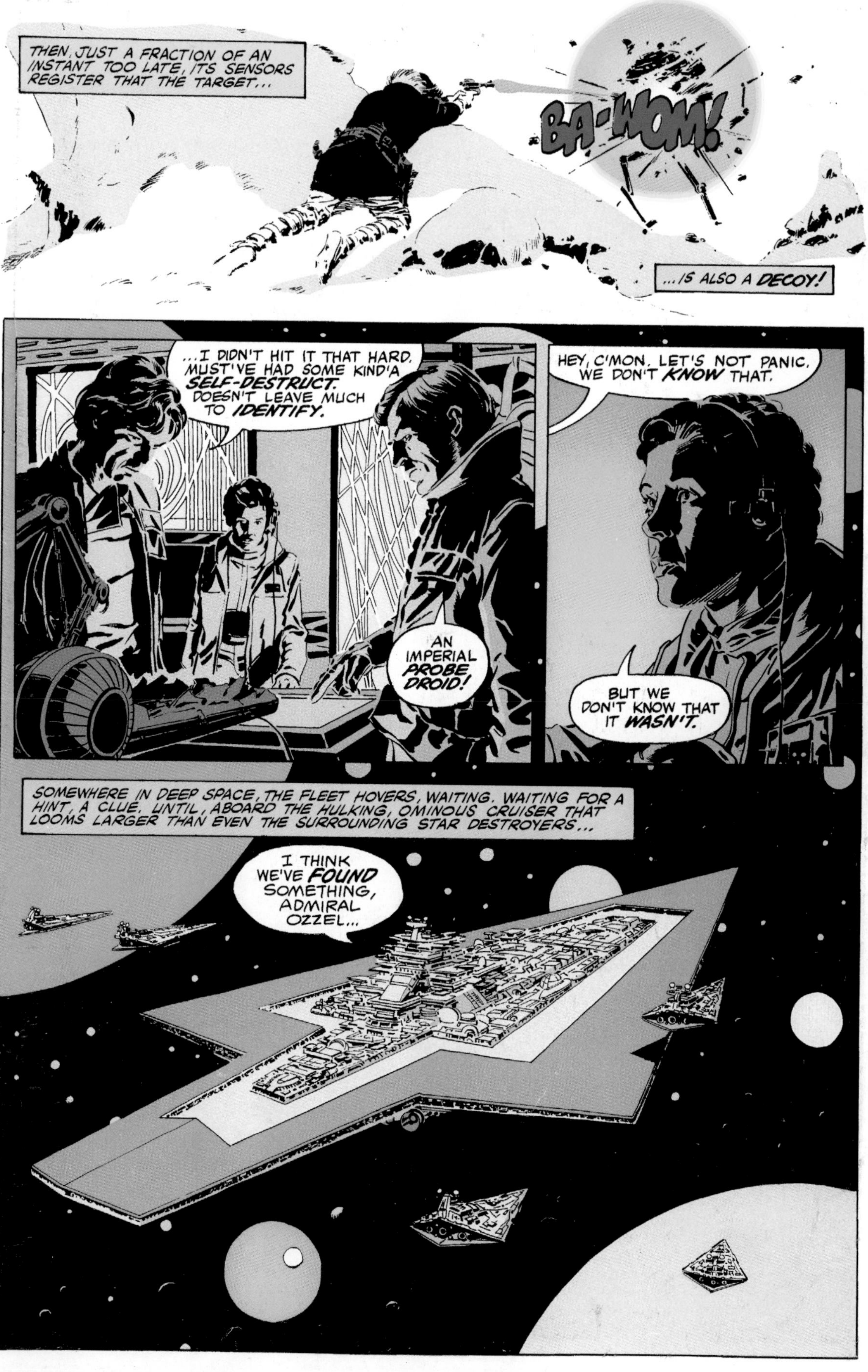

THEN, JUST A FRACTION OF AN INSTANT TOO LATE, ITS SENSORS REGISTER THAT THE TARGET...
BA-WOM!
...IS ALSO A DECOY!
...I DIDN'T HIT IT THAT HARD. MUST'VE HAD SOME KIND'A SELF-DESTRUCT. DOESN'T LEAVE MUCH TO IDENTIFY.
AN IMPERIAL PROBE DROID!
HEY, C'MON. LET'S NOT PANIC. WE DON'T KNOW THAT.
BUT WE DON'T KNOW THAT IT WASN'T.
SOMEWHERE IN DEEP SPACE, THE FLEET HOVERS, WAITING. WAITING FOR A HINT, A CLUE. UNTIL, ABOARD THE HULKING, OMINOUS CRUISER THAT LOOMS LARGER THAN EVEN THE SURROUNDING STAR DESTROYERS...
I THINK WE'VE FOUND SOMETHING, ADMIRAL OZZEL...

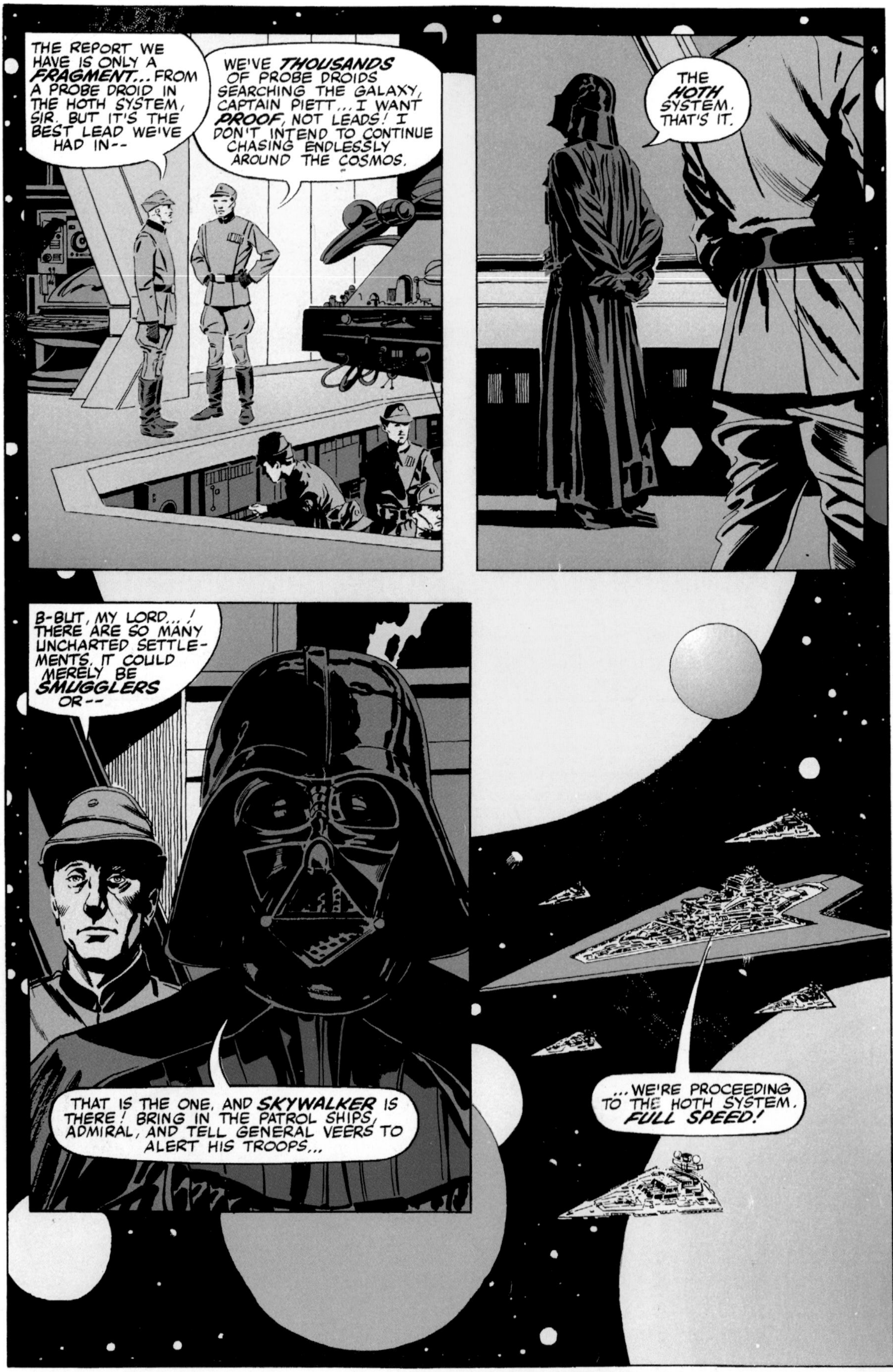
THE REPORT WE HAVE IS ONLY A FRAGMENT... FROM A PROBE DROID IN THE HOTH SYSTEM, SIR. BUT IT'S THE BEST LEAD WE'VE HAD IN--
WE'VE THOUSANDS OF PROBE DROIDS SEARCHING THE GALAXY, CAPTAIN PIETT... I WANT PROOF, NOT LEADS! I DON'T INTEND TO CONTINUE CHASING ENDLESSLY AROUND THE COSMOS.
THE HOTH SYSTEM. THAT'S IT.
B-BUT, MY LORD...! THERE ARE SO MANY UNCHARTED SETTLE-MENTS. IT COULD MERELY BE SMUGGLERS OR--
THAT IS THE ONE, AND SKYWALKER IS THERE! BRING IN THE PATROL SHIPS, ADMIRAL, AND TELL GENERAL VEERS TO ALERT HIS TROOPS...
...WE'RE PROCEEDING TO THE HOTH SYSTEM. FULL SPEED!

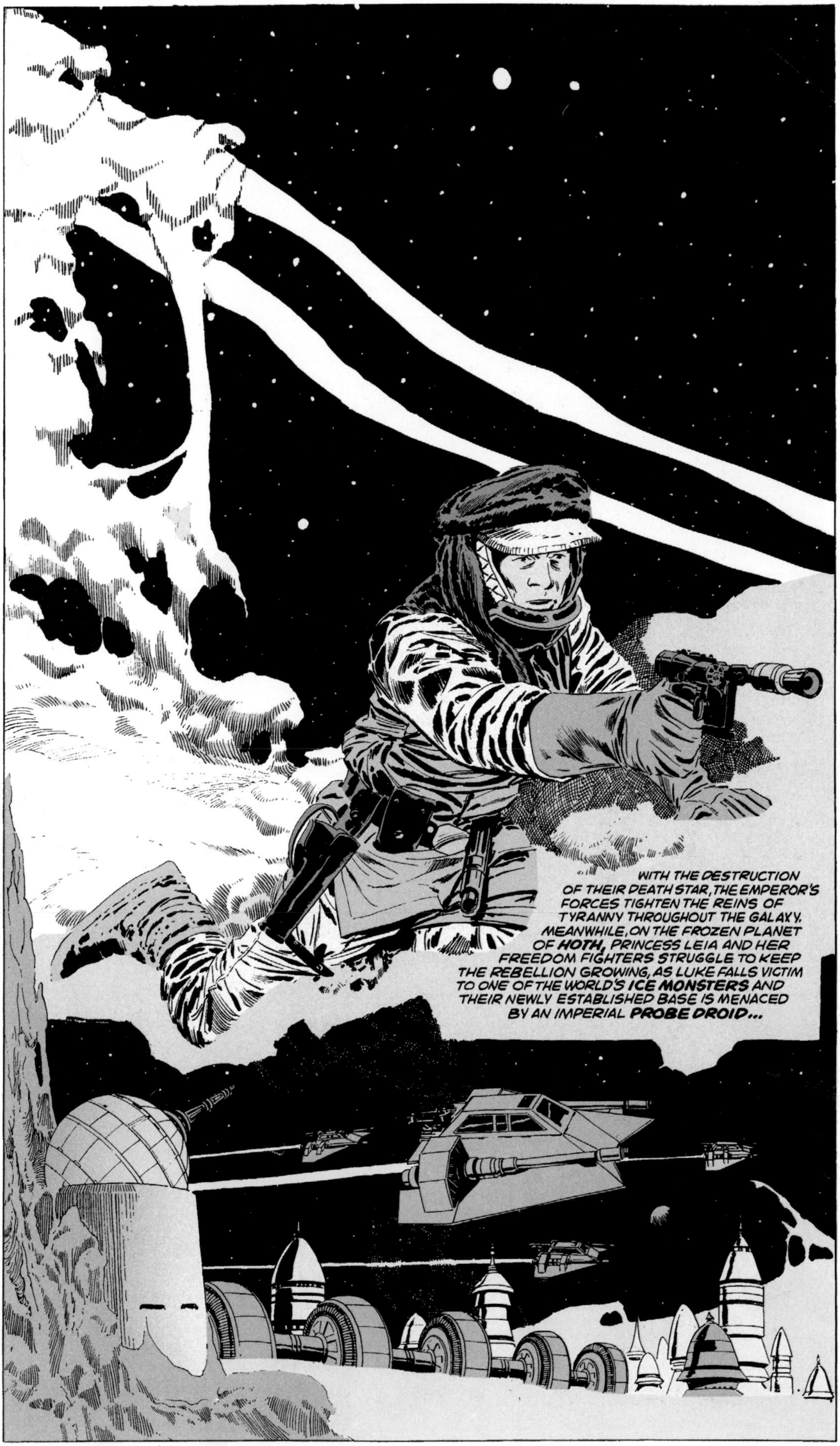
WITH THE DESTRUCTION OF THEIR DEATH STAR, THE EMPEROR'S FORCES TIGHTEN THE REINS OF TYRANNY THROUGHOUT THE GALAXY. MEANWHILE, ON THE FROZEN PLANET OF HOTH, PRINCESS LEIA AND HER FREEDOM FIGHTERS STRUGGLE TO KEEP THE REBELLION GROWING, AS LUKE FALLS VICTIM TO ONE OF THE WORLD'S ICE MONSTERS AND THEIR NEWLY ESTABLISHED BASE IS MENACED BY AN IMPERIAL PROBE DROID...

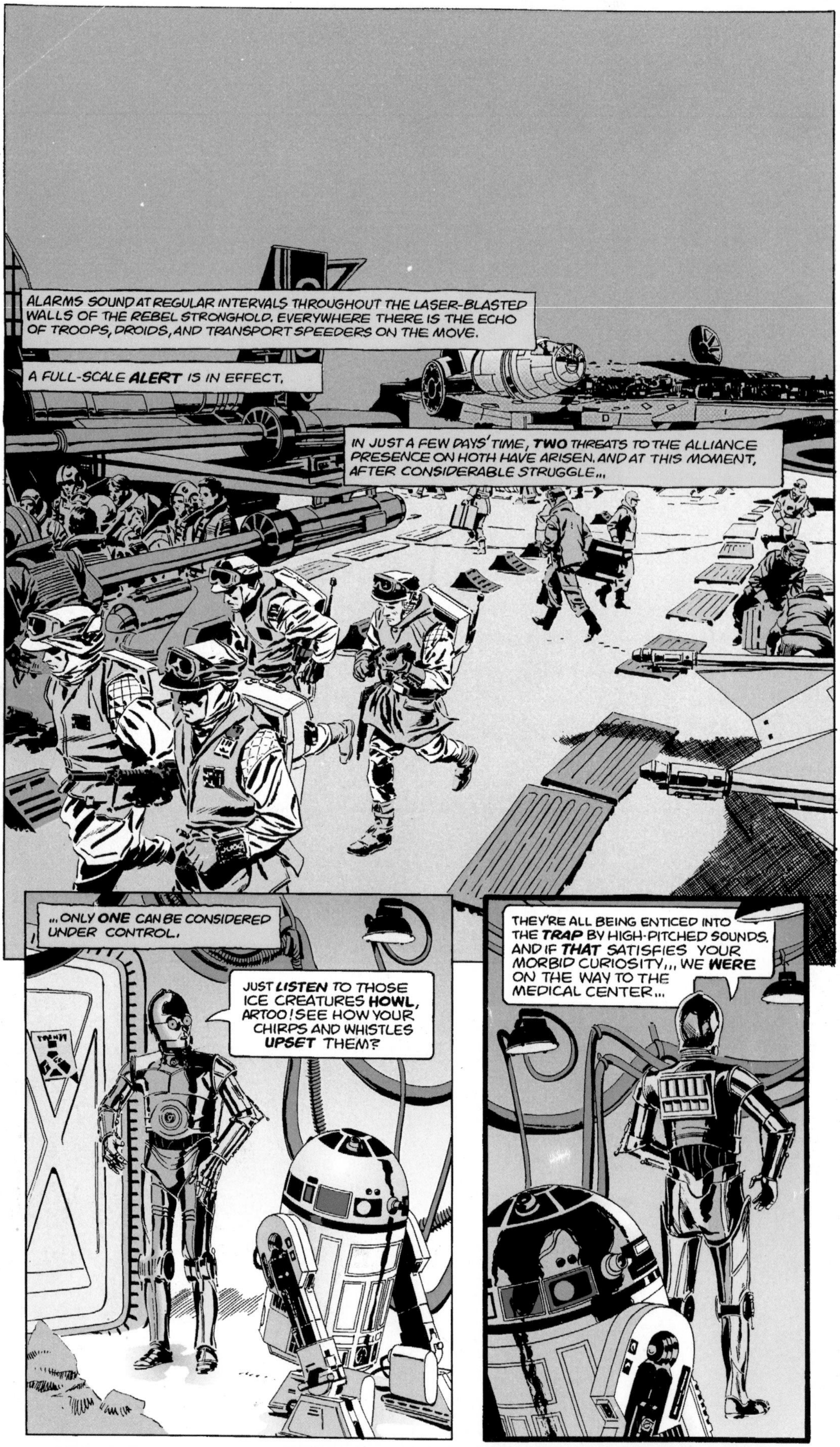
ALARMS SOUND AT REGULAR INTERVALS THROUGHOUT THE LASER-BLASTED WALLS OF THE REBEL STRONGHOLD. EVERYWHERE THERE IS THE ECHO OF TROOPS, DROIDS, AND TRANSPORT SPEEDERS ON THE MOVE.
A FULL-SCALE ALERT IS IN EFFECT.
IN JUST A FEW DAYS' TIME, TWO THREATS TO THE ALLIANCE PRESENCE ON HOTH HAVE ARISEN. AND AT THIS MOMENT, AFTER CONSIDERABLE STRUGGLE...
...ONLY ONE CAN BE CONSIDERED UNDER CONTROL.
JUST LISTEN TO THOSE ICE CREATURES HOWL, ARTOO! SEE HOW YOUR CHIRPS AND WHISTLES UPSET THEM?
THEY'RE ALL BEING ENTICED INTO THE TRAP BY HIGH-PITCHED SOUNDS. AND IF THAT SATISFIES YOUR MORBID CURIOSITY... WE WERE ON THE WAY TO THE MEDICAL CENTER...

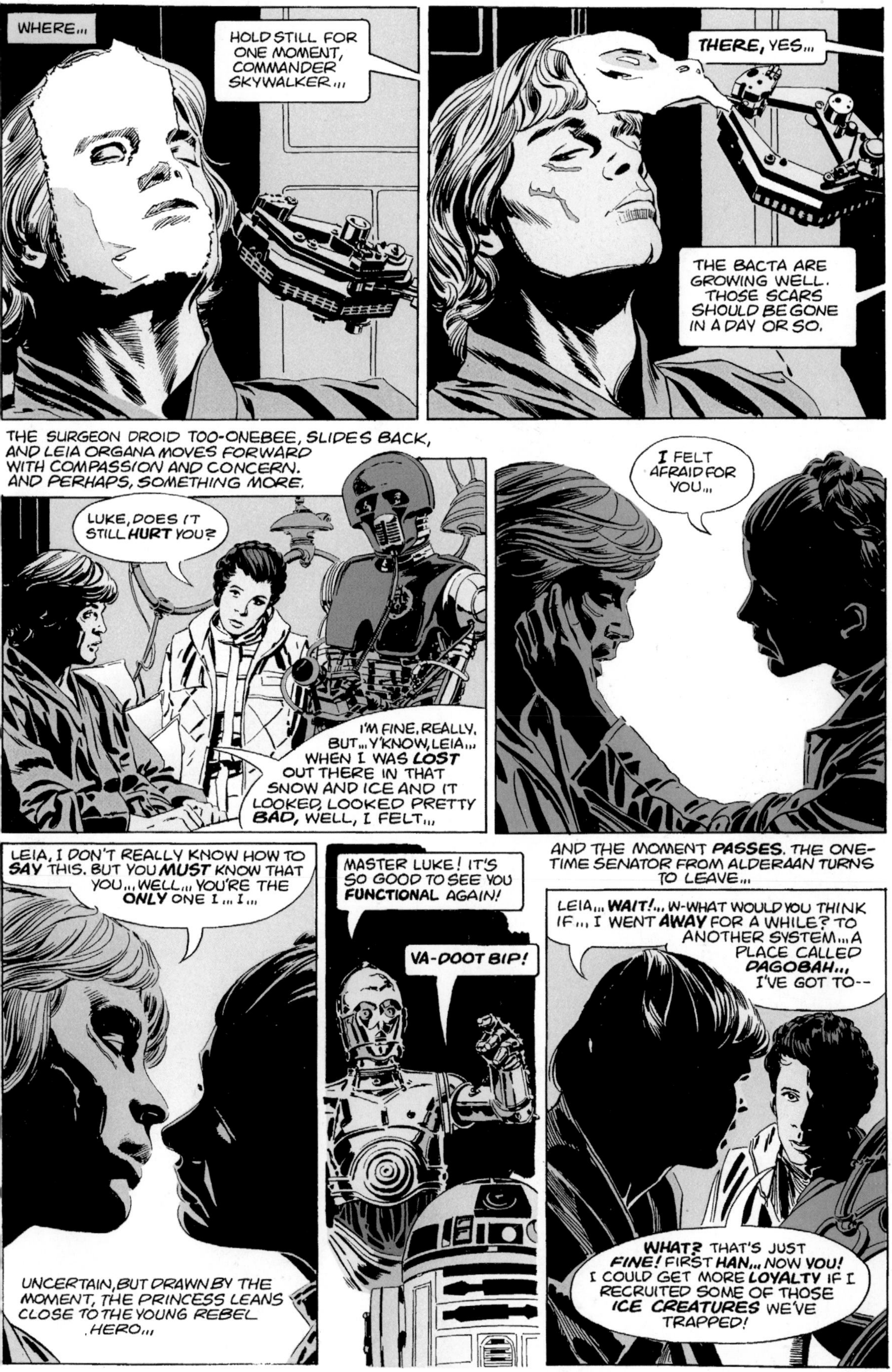
WHERE...
HOLD STILL FOR ONE MOMENT, COMMANDER SKYWALKER...
THERE, YES...
THE BACTA ARE GROWING WELL. THOSE SCARS SHOULD BE GONE IN A DAY OR SO.
THE SURGEON DROID TOO-ONEBEE, SLIDES BACK, AND LEIA ORGANA MOVES FORWARD WITH COMPASSION AND CONCERN. AND PERHAPS, SOMETHING MORE.
LUKE, DOES IT STILL HURT YOU?
I'M FINE, REALLY, BUT... Y'KNOW, LEIA... WHEN I WAS LOST OUT THERE IN THAT SNOW AND ICE AND IT LOOKED, LOOKED PRETTY BAD, WELL, I FELT...
I FELT AFRAID FOR YOU...
LEIA, I DON'T REALLY KNOW HOW TO SAY THIS. BUT YOU MUST KNOW THAT YOU... WELL... YOU'RE THE ONLY ONE I ... I...
UNCERTAIN, BUT DRAWN BY THE MOMENT, THE PRINCESS LEANS CLOSE TO THE YOUNG REBEL HERO...
MASTER LUKE! IT'S SO GOOD TO SEE YOU FUNCTIONAL AGAIN!
VA-DOOT BIP!
AND THE MOMENT PASSES. THE ONE-TIME SENATOR FROM ALDERAAN TURNS TO LEAVE...
LEIA... WAIT!... W-WHAT WOULD YOU THINK IF... I WENT AWAY FOR A WHILE? TO ANOTHER SYSTEM... A PLACE CALLED DAGOBAH..., I'VE GOT TO--
WHAT? THAT'S JUST FINE! FIRST HAN... NOW YOU! I COULD GET MORE LOYALTY IF I RECRUITED SOME OF THOSE ICE CREATURES WE'VE TRAPPED!

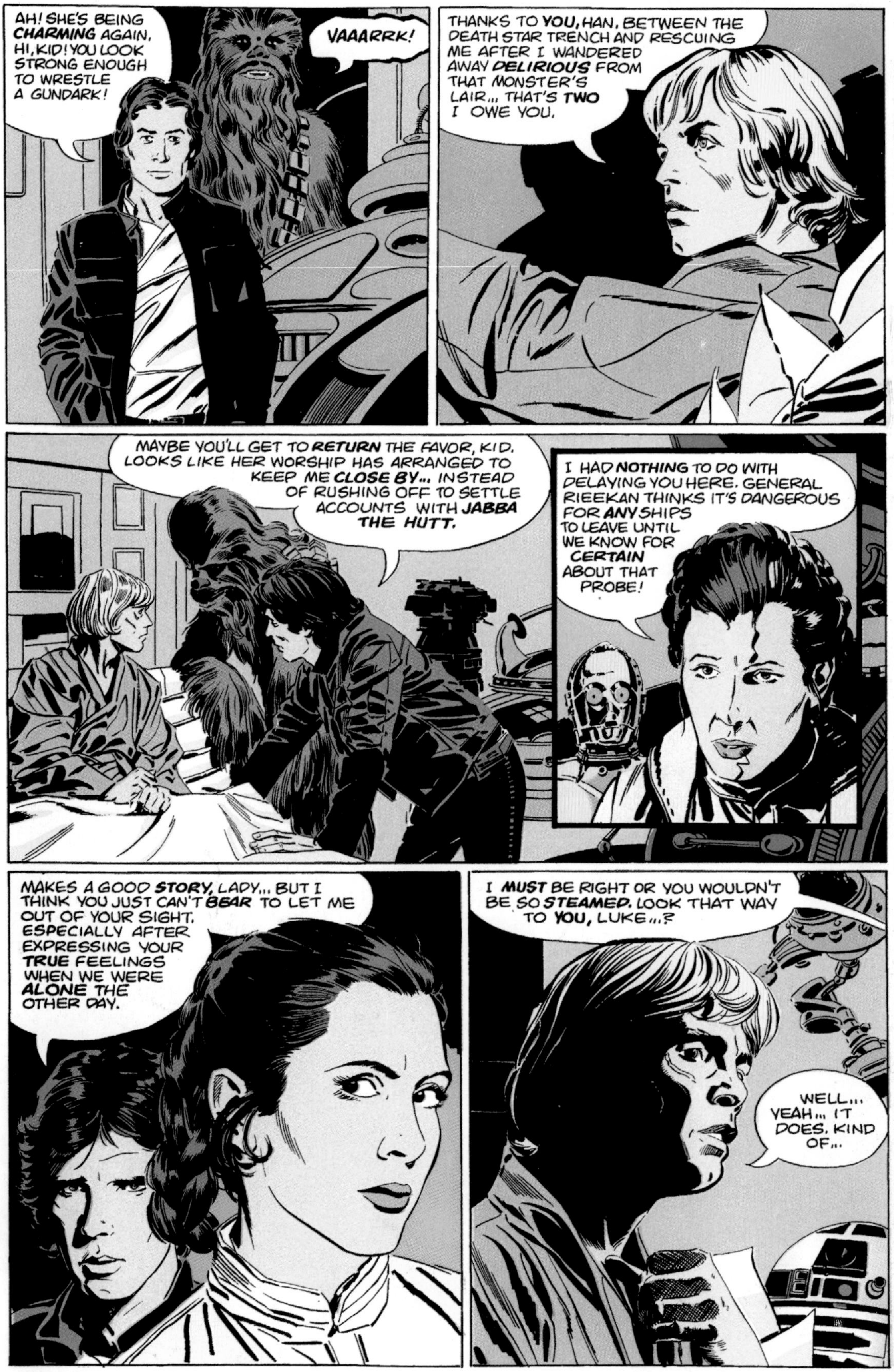
AH! SHE'S BEING CHARMING AGAIN. HI, KID! YOU LOOK STRONG ENOUGH TO WRESTLE A GUNDARK!
VAAARRK!
THANKS TO YOU, HAN. BETWEEN THE DEATH STAR TRENCH AND RESCUING ME AFTER I WANDERED AWAY DELIRIOUS FROM THAT MONSTER'S LAIR... THAT'S TWO I OWE YOU.
MAYBE YOU'LL GET TO RETURN THE FAVOR, KID. LOOKS LIKE HER WORSHIP HAS ARRANGED TO KEEP ME CLOSE BY... INSTEAD OF RUSHING OFF TO SETTLE ACCOUNTS WITH JABBA THE HUTT.
I HAD NOTHING TO DO WITH DELAYING YOU HERE. GENERAL RIEEKAN THINKS IT'S DANGEROUS FOR ANY SHIPS TO LEAVE UNTIL WE KNOW FOR CERTAIN ABOUT THAT PROBE!
MAKES A GOOD STORY, LADY... BUT I THINK YOU JUST CAN'T BEAR TO LET ME OUT OF YOUR SIGHT. ESPECIALLY AFTER EXPRESSING YOUR TRUE FEELINGS WHEN WE WERE ALONE THE OTHER DAY.
I MUST BE RIGHT OR YOU WOULDN'T BE SO STEAMED. LOOK THAT WAY TO YOU, LUKE...?
WELL... YEAH... IT DOES. KIND OF...

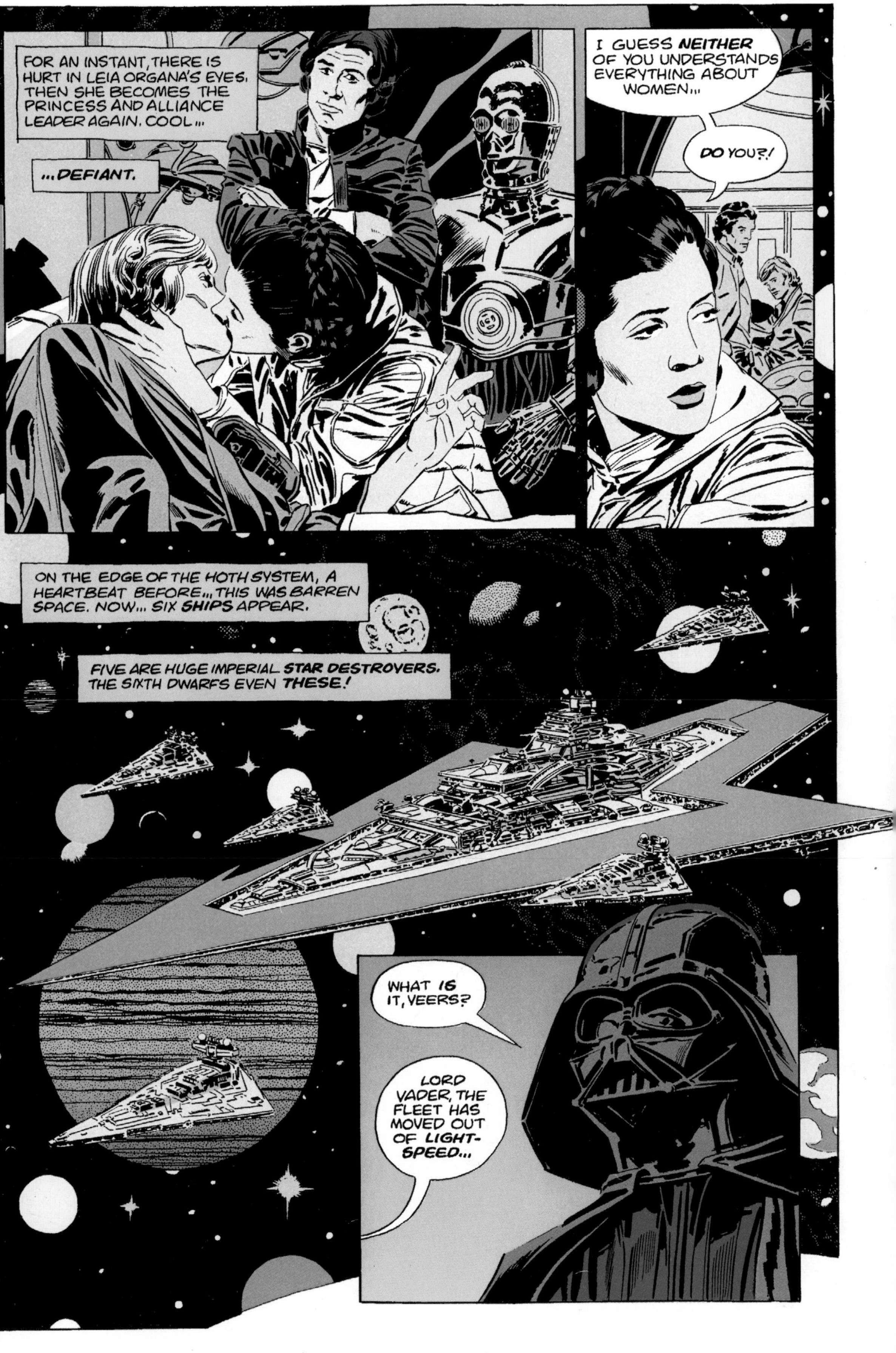
FOR AN INSTANT, THERE IS HURT IN LEIA ORGANA'S EYES. THEN SHE BECOMES THE PRINCESS AND ALLIANCE LEADER AGAIN. COOL...
...DEFIANT.
I GUESS NEITHER OF YOU UNDERSTANDS EVERYTHING ABOUT WOMEN...
DO YOU?!
ON THE EDGE OF THE HOTH SYSTEM, A HEARTBEAT BEFORE... THIS WAS BARREN SPACE. NOW... SIX SHIPS APPEAR.
FIVE ARE HUGE IMPERIAL STAR DESTROYERS. THE SIXTH DWARFS EVEN THESE!
WHAT IS IT, VEERS?
LORD VADER, THE FLEET HAS MOVED OUT OF LIGHT-SPEED...

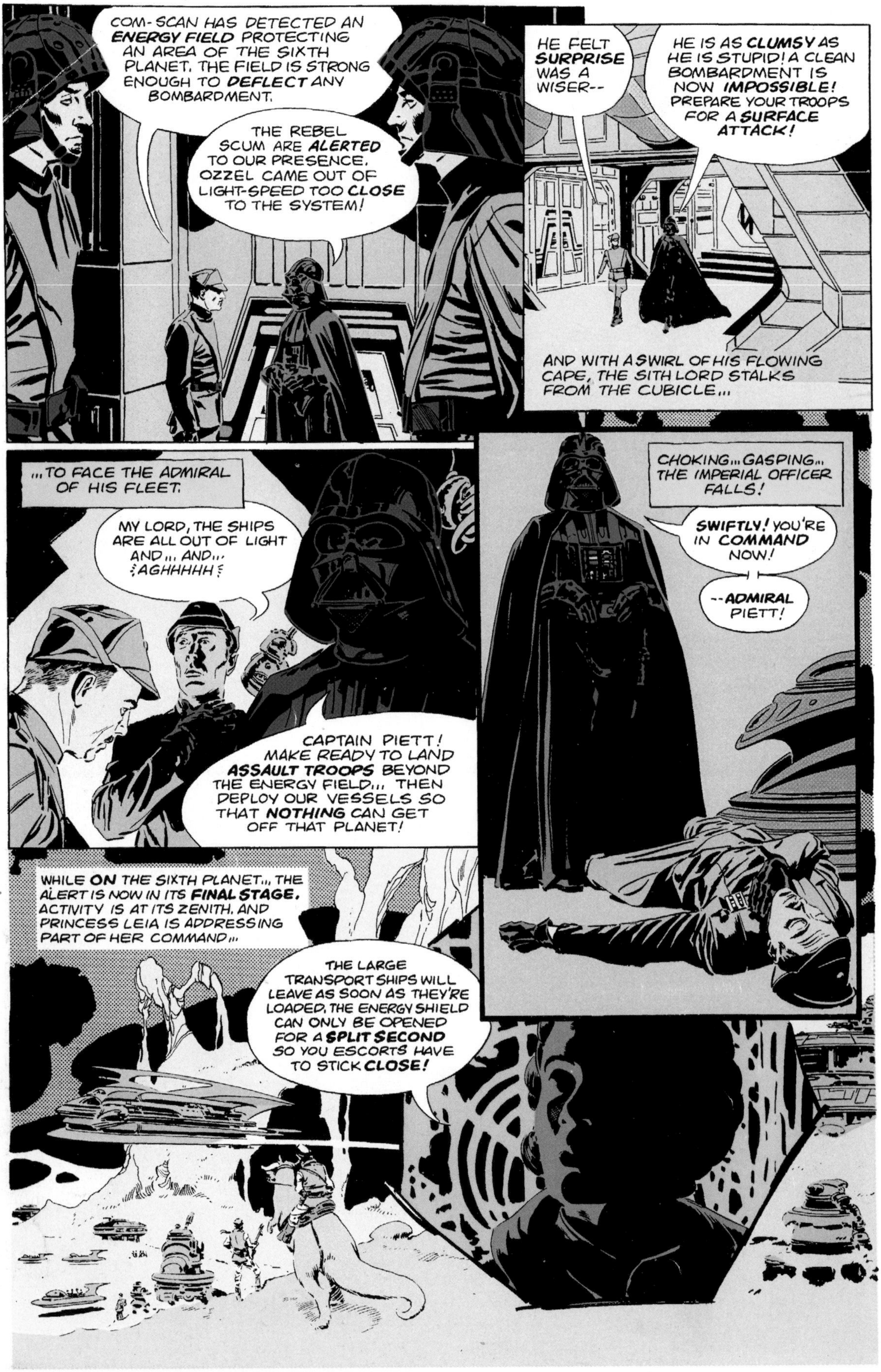
COM-SCAN HAS DETECTED AN ENERGY FIELD PROTECTING AN AREA OF THE SIXTH PLANET. THE FIELD IS STRONG ENOUGH TO DEFLECT ANY BOMBARDMENT.
THE REBEL SCUM ARE ALERTED TO OUR PRESENCE. OZZEL CAME OUT OF LIGHT-SPEED TOO CLOSE TO THE SYSTEM!
HE FELT SURPRISE WAS A WISER--
HE IS AS CLUMSY AS HE IS STUPID! A CLEAN BOMBARDMENT IS NOW IMPOSSIBLE! PREPARE YOUR TROOPS FOR A SURFACE ATTACK!
AND WITH A SWIRL OF HIS FLOWING CAPE, THE SITH LORD STALKS FROM THE CUBICLE...
...TO FACE THE ADMIRAL OF HIS FLEET.
MY LORD, THE SHIPS ARE ALL OUT OF LIGHT AND... AND... AGHHHHH
CAPTAIN PIETT! MAKE READY TO LAND ASSAULT TROOPS BEYOND THE ENERGY FIELD... THEN DEPLOY OUR VESSELS SO THAT NOTHING CAN GET OFF THAT PLANET!
CHOKING... GASPING... THE IMPERIAL OFFICER FALLS!
SWIFTLY! YOU'RE IN COMMAND NOW!
--ADMIRAL PIETT!
WHILE ON THE SIXTH PLANET... THE ALERT IS NOW IN ITS FINAL STAGE. ACTIVITY IS AT ITS ZENITH, AND PRINCESS LEIA IS ADDRESSING PART OF HER COMMAND...
THE LARGE TRANSPORT SHIPS WILL LEAVE AS SOON AS THEY'RE LOADED. THE ENERGY SHIELD CAN ONLY BE OPENED FOR A SPLIT SECOND SO YOU ESCORTS HAVE TO STICK CLOSE!

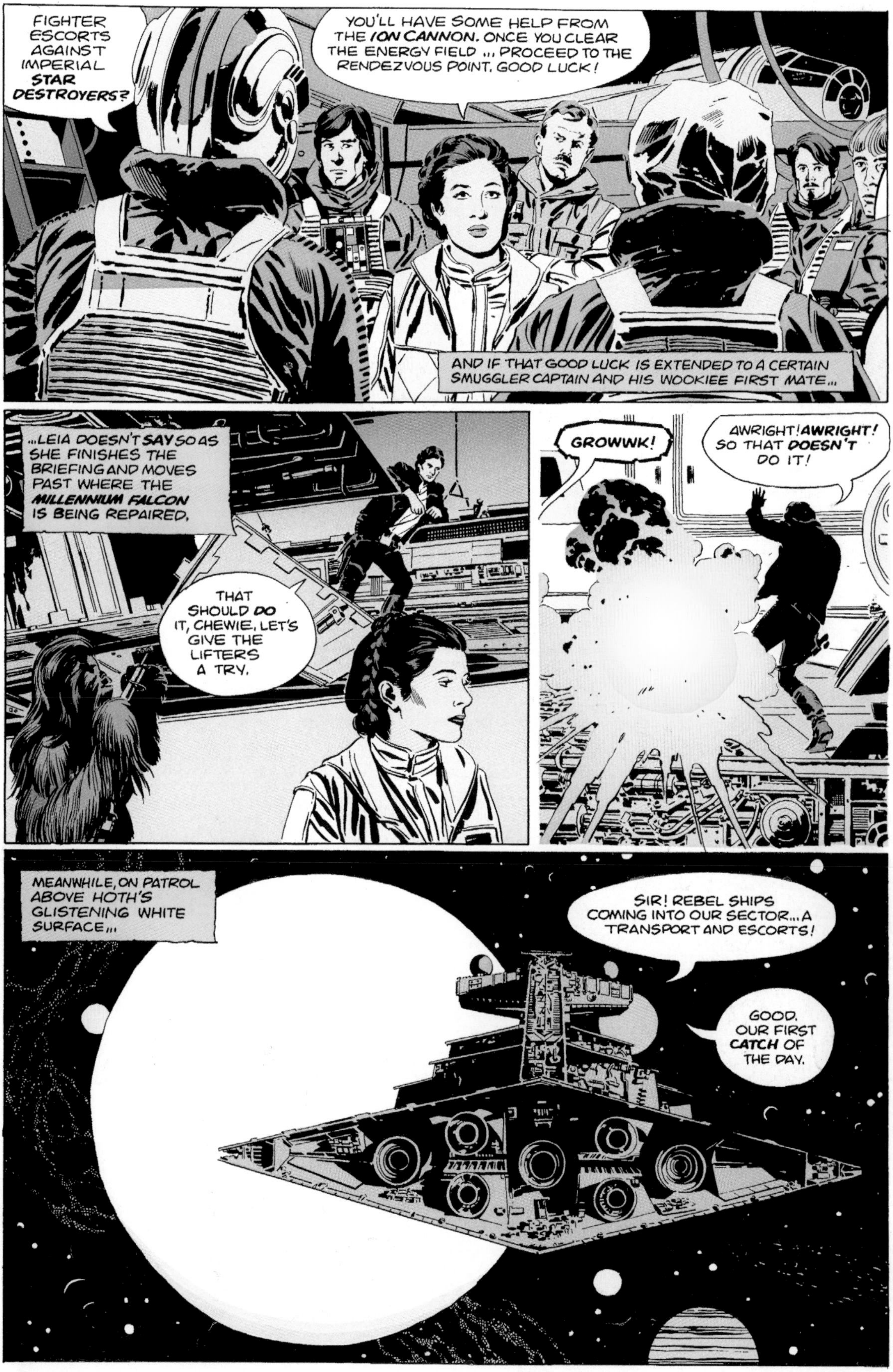
FIGHTER ESCORTS AGAINST IMPERIAL STAR DESTROYERS?
YOU'LL HAVE SOME HELP FROM THE ION CANNON. ONCE YOU CLEAR THE ENERGY FIELD ... PROCEED TO THE RENDEZVOUS POINT. GOOD LUCK!
AND IF THAT GOOD LUCK IS EXTENDED TO A CERTAIN SMUGGLER CAPTAIN AND HIS WOOKIEE FIRST MATE...
...LEIA DOESN'T SAY SO AS SHE FINISHES THE BRIEFING AND MOVES PAST WHERE THE MILLENNIUM FALCON IS BEING REPAIRED.
THAT SHOULD DO IT, CHEWIE. LET'S GIVE THE LIFTERS A TRY.
GROWWK!
AWRIGHT! AWRIGHT! SO THAT DOESN'T DO IT!
MEANWHILE, ON PATROL ABOVE HOTH'S GLISTENING WHITE SURFACE...
SIR! REBEL SHIPS COMING INTO OUR SECTOR... A TRANSPORT AND ESCORTS!
GOOD. OUR FIRST CATCH OF THE DAY.

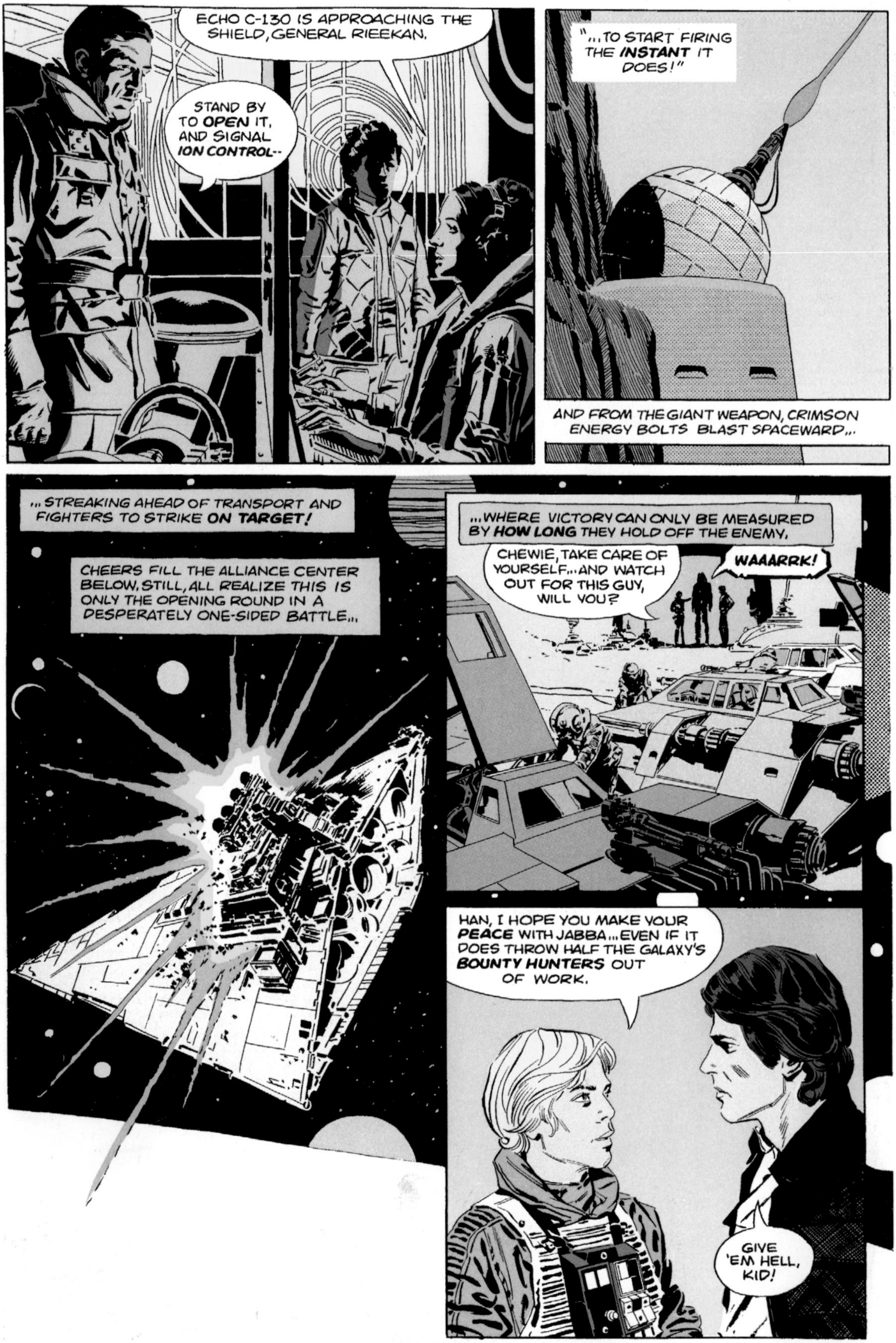

ECHO C-130 IS APPROACHING THE SHIELD, GENERAL RIEEKAN.
STAND BY TO **OPEN** IT, AND SIGNAL **ION CONTROL**--
"...TO START FIRING THE **INSTANT** IT DOES!"
AND FROM THE GIANT WEAPON, CRIMSON ENERGY BOLTS BLAST SPACEWARD...
...STREAKING AHEAD OF TRANSPORT AND FIGHTERS TO STRIKE **ON TARGET!**
CHEERS FILL THE ALLIANCE CENTER BELOW. STILL, ALL REALIZE THIS IS ONLY THE OPENING ROUND IN A DESPERATELY ONE-SIDED BATTLE...
...WHERE VICTORY CAN ONLY BE MEASURED BY **HOW LONG** THEY HOLD OFF THE ENEMY.
CHEWIE, TAKE CARE OF YOURSELF...AND WATCH OUT FOR THIS GUY, WILL YOU?
WAAARRK!
HAN, I HOPE YOU MAKE YOUR **PEACE** WITH JABBA...EVEN IF IT DOES THROW HALF THE GALAXY'S **BOUNTY HUNTERS** OUT OF WORK.
GIVE 'EM HELL, KID!

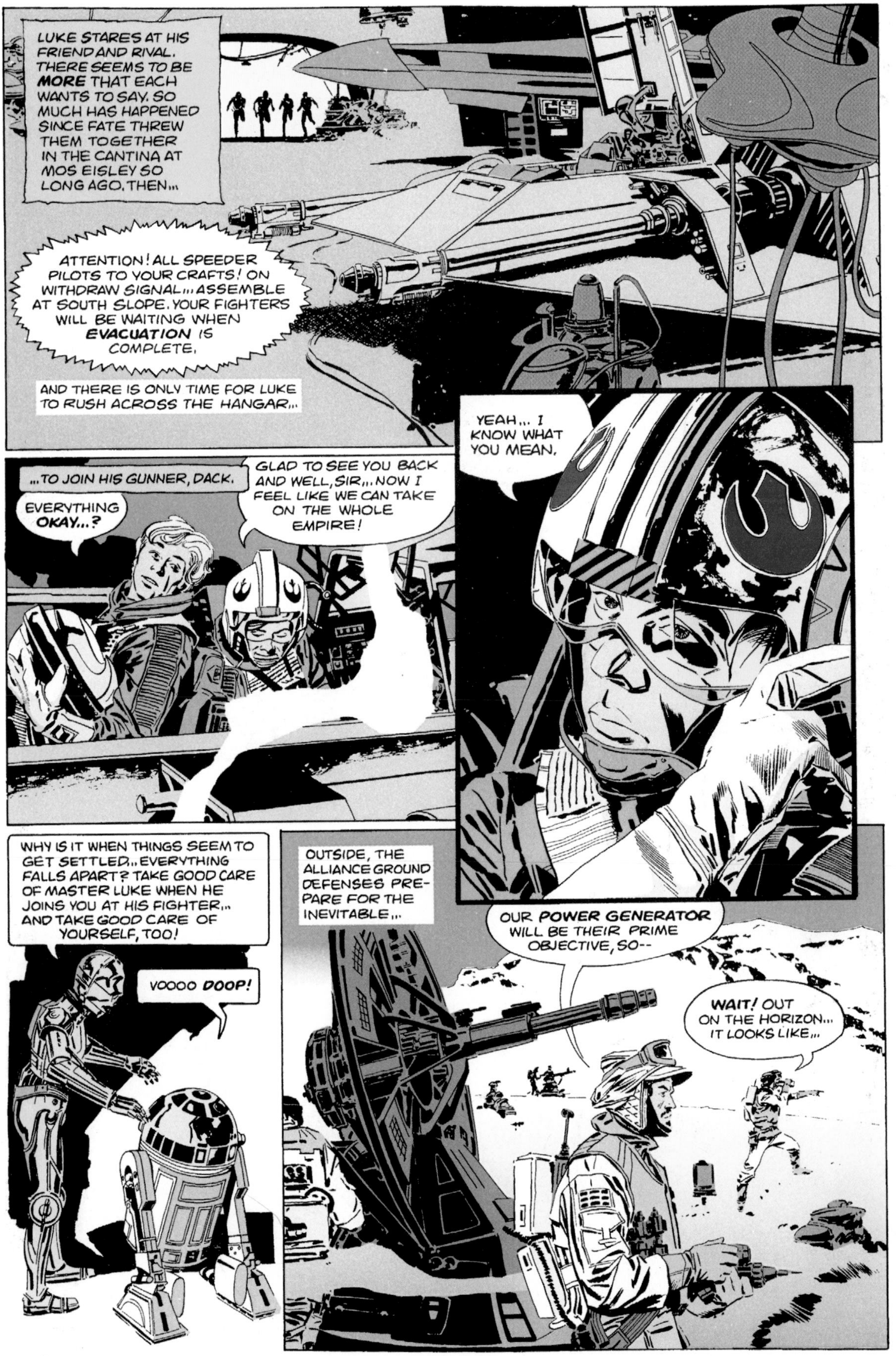

LUKE STARES AT HIS FRIEND AND RIVAL. THERE SEEMS TO BE **MORE** THAT EACH WANTS TO SAY. SO MUCH HAS HAPPENED SINCE FATE THREW THEM TOGETHER IN THE CANTINA AT MOS EISLEY SO LONG AGO. THEN...
ATTENTION! ALL SPEEDER PILOTS TO YOUR CRAFTS! ON WITHDRAW SIGNAL... ASSEMBLE AT SOUTH SLOPE. YOUR FIGHTERS WILL BE WAITING WHEN **EVACUATION** IS COMPLETE.
AND THERE IS ONLY TIME FOR LUKE TO RUSH ACROSS THE HANGAR...
...TO JOIN HIS GUNNER, DACK.
EVERYTHING **OKAY...?**
GLAD TO SEE YOU BACK AND WELL, SIR... NOW I FEEL LIKE WE CAN TAKE ON THE WHOLE EMPIRE!
YEAH... I KNOW WHAT YOU MEAN.
WHY IS IT WHEN THINGS SEEM TO GET SETTLED... EVERYTHING FALLS APART? TAKE GOOD CARE OF MASTER LUKE WHEN HE JOINS YOU AT HIS FIGHTER... AND TAKE GOOD CARE OF YOURSELF, TOO!
VOOOO **DOOP!**
OUTSIDE, THE ALLIANCE GROUND DEFENSES PRE-PARE FOR THE INEVITABLE...
OUR **POWER GENERATOR** WILL BE THEIR PRIME OBJECTIVE, SO--
WAIT! OUT ON THE HORIZON... IT LOOKS LIKE...

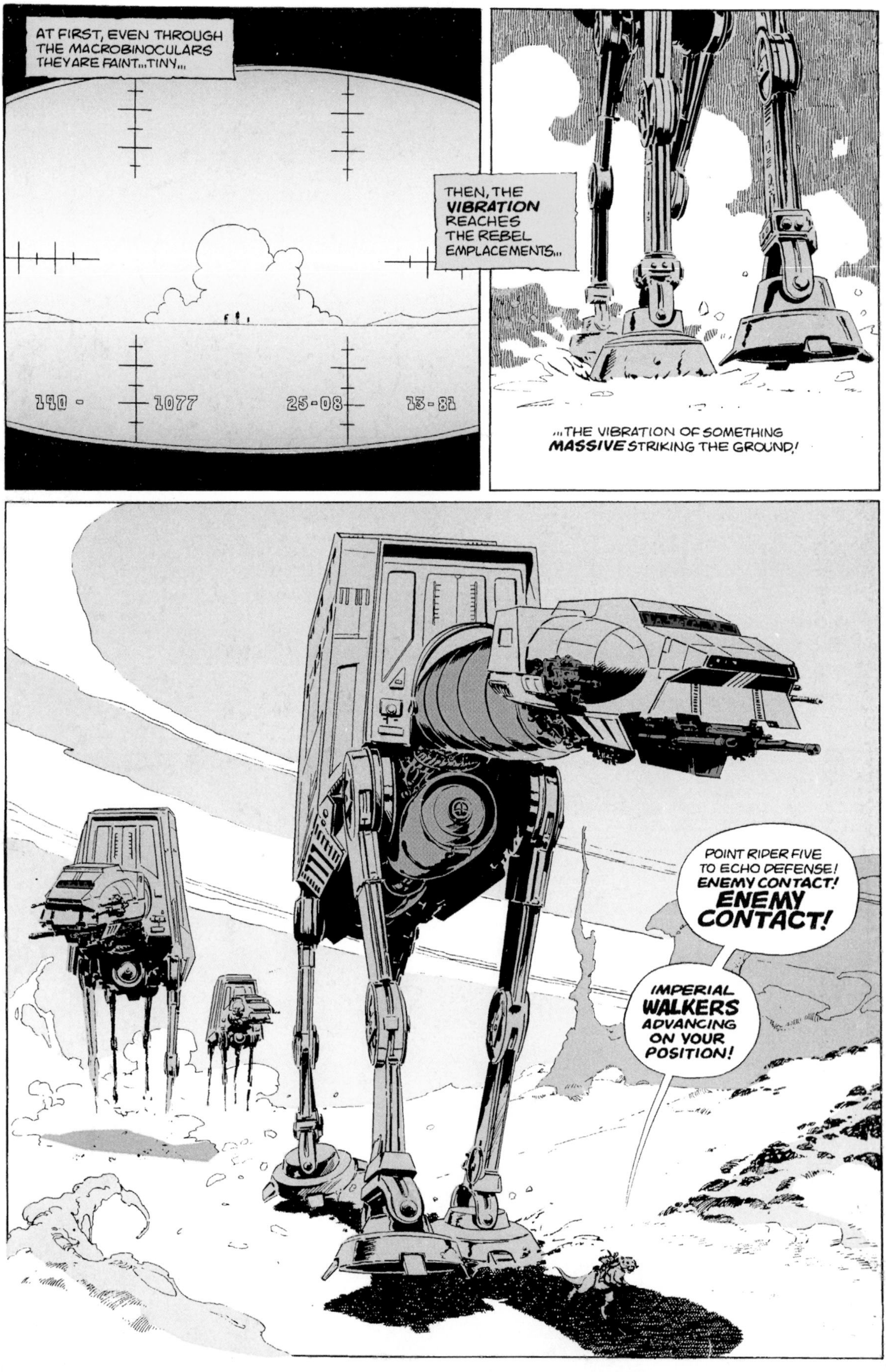
AT FIRST, EVEN THROUGH THE MACROBINOCULARS THEY ARE FAINT... TINY...
140 -
1077
25-08
13-81
THEN, THE VIBRATION REACHES THE REBEL EMPLACEMENTS...
...THE VIBRATION OF SOMETHING MASSIVE STRIKING THE GROUND!
POINT RIDER FIVE TO ECHO DEFENSE! ENEMY CONTACT! ENEMY CONTACT!
IMPERIAL WALKERS ADVANCING ON YOUR POSITION!